PRAISE FOR MICKEY FRIEDMAN

"She knows how to create that sense of place which is so important to any novel but particularly to crime fiction; her characters are believable, her mystery is credible."

P. D. James

"What an extraordinarily skillful and intelligent and interesting novelist she is."

Alice Adams

"My current favorite suspense story writer."

Judith Rossner

"Mickey Friedman is wonderful."

Susan Isaacs

Also by Mickey Friedman
Published by Ballantine Books:

HURRICANE SEASON

THE FAULT TREE

PAPER PHOENIX

Mickey Friedman

BALLANTINE BOOKS • NEW YORK

Library of Congress Catalog Card Number: 85-20696

ISBN 0-345-33676-3

This edition published by arrangement with E.P. Dutton

Publisher's Note: This novel is a work of fiction. Names, characters,
places, and incidents are either the product of the author's imagination or
are used fictitiously, and any resemblance to actual persons, living or dead,
events, or locales is entirely coincidental.

Manufactured in the United States of America

First Ballantine Books Edition: March 1987

TO COLLIN WILCOX

ONE

Until Richard left me, I had never thought much about murder. After he left me, I thought about it a great deal. Being abandoned by your husband when you've just turned forty-four is enough to make any woman consider violence, and being abandoned for a law student almost exactly twenty years your junior is a situation begging for mayhem.

But violence in the abstract, such as a satisfying fantasy of beating Richard bloody, is a long way from the real thing. Larry Hawkins's death and its aftermath taught me that, and a good deal more besides, at a time when I imagined I had very little left to learn.

The popular wisdom of the moment said that I was OK and you were OK. I could go only halfway with that. I *was* OK, or I had done my best to be. I had been faithful, supportive, loyal, an ornament to Richard's career. I had gotten myself on committees of various cultural and philanthropic organizations and willed myself to care about their projects. I had sat through political dinners, my eyes watering with cigar smoke and suppressed yawns, when I would've preferred being at home with a good book. I had been pretty close to OK.

Nothing could convince me, on the other hand, that you were OK, if "you" meant Richard. Because to kick a perfectly OK wife in her stylish-but-not-so-flashy posterior is not OK and never will be, no matter what writers sympathetic to the problems of the male menopause say.

I thought about murder. When Richard closed the door

behind him, my career as Mrs. Richard Longstreet, San Francisco Big Shot, was officially over. I was left with a renovated and rapidly appreciating pre-Earthquake cottage on Lake Street with a dining table at which the mayor would never again have dinner. The curtain had descended, and I was left in the dark backstage with the sudden suspicion that my big scenes had already been played.

A difficult situation was made more difficult by the fact that 1975, the year of Richard's defection, was also the year that San Francisco—or, perhaps more accurately, the San Francisco press—discovered older women. In previous times, we females had marked the passing years in relative tranquility. Now, we were in ferment. At the age of forty-four, fifty-four, sixty-four, we were retreading ourselves for the job market, taking assertiveness training, petitioning our congressmen. We were banding together and starting cute new restaurants. We were learning carpentry and setting up communes on rolling acreage north of the city, where we birthed calves, walked around in mud-splattered hip boots, and lived in raw redwood cabins with no indoor plumbing. We were on the move.

I wasn't going anywhere. Sitting in my glass-enclosed sun porch overlooking Mountain Lake Park, I would drop the paper beside my chair and watch the winter rain batter the weaving branches of the almond tree. When I got tired of doing that I would take a pill and lie down.

Since I wasn't ready for calf-birthing, I had, as I saw it at the time, three possibilities: dye my hair, take a cruise, or commit suicide.

I decided against dying my hair. Even with a little gray here and there the chestnut was holding its own. After briefer consideration I also dismissed cosmetic nips and tucks on the eyelids and jawline. "You have good bones, Maggie," my mother used to say, comforting me for being too thin. By this time I was glad. The less flesh, the fewer possibilities for sagging. My chin was a bit sharper than when I was twenty, and my eyes (the color of apple-green jade, Richard had rhapsodized in happier days) had seen a lot more, but I'd continue without chemical or surgical intervention. If Richard had chosen to see me, his domestic reflection, as on the verge of decay, that was his problem.

No cruise, either. I wasn't ready to fend off the attentions of vacationing liquor salesmen whose wives were confined to the cabin with a touch of *mal de mer,* and playing shuffleboard with other fun-loving divorcées didn't appeal to me either. What I dreaded most was the thought that I'd probably fling myself at some greasy-haired ship's vocalist wearing a diamond pinky ring and, worst of all, be rejected by him.

Suicide was my last option. I finally nixed it because I was too damn mad at Richard to give him the satisfaction. He would have played the scene well. His gray hair and elongated face gave him an attenuated, spiritual look that his black suit set off wonderfully. He would have stood, to all appearances guilt-ridden and grief-stricken, at my bier, and every woman at the service would have thought he looked worth committing suicide over. And underneath it all, he would have felt nothing.

If Larry Hawkins hadn't died, I might never have taken off my salmon-colored peignoir again. Looking back, it seems that I wore it all day, every day, for months. That can't be true, because I am fairly meticulous, and must have laundered it occasionally. I don't remember. In fact, I remember very little of that time. I moved through the days like a salmon-colored blur, soft around the edges and the center completely dissolved, like a piece of chocolate candy that's been left in the sun. Or like my marriage. My marriage had dissolved, too. That's why they call it "dissolution of marriage," I reasoned in my befuddled way. My brain didn't work so well in those days, because I was taking a great many pills.

There was a pill in the morning, to calm my system down from the shock of getting out of bed. Then one at noon, to prepare me for my afternoon nap. At bedtime there had to be another to assure me of a good night's sleep. Those were the regulars. If I started feeling jumpy in between, or burned the toast, or got a phone call from my lawyer, it was reason enough to take another. I was turning into a dissolving, salmon-colored junkie.

This situation continued from before Christmas to early March. How long it might have gone on I don't know. I suppose I could still be stumbling around the house, subsisting on canned soup and staring moodily at whatever happened to be on television, if I hadn't been awakened one afternoon by the sound of the newspaper slapping against the front steps.

It was four o'clock, and I had been sleeping since one. From what I had seen out the windows, it had been a glorious early-spring day—the sky a profound California blue, the park meadow the daisy-spangled bright green that comes after periodic hard drenching. Through the branches of the almond tree, now furred with delicate white blossoms, I had seen some neighborhood athletes braving the muddy parcourse. Then I had gone to sleep. When the thump of the paper penetrated my stupor I opened my eyes and watched the patterns the lowering sun was making on the bedspread of the king-sized bed in which I lay, still habituated, on my accustomed half.

The *Herald*. For once the delivery boy hit the steps, instead of the Japanese magnolia tree next to them, or the slick-leaved boxwood bushes at the bottom. What time was it? I was distinctly put out. The newsboy's accuracy had robbed me of another half hour to forty-five minutes of sleep, which would have meant my waking just in time to start thinking about which Campbell's production to have for dinner. Now, it was too early.

When each minute of consciousness is a burden, an extra forty-five of them constituted an almost insurmountable tragedy. What in hell would I do until dinnertime? I concentrated, watching the motes of dust spinning slowly in the ray of sunlight that had slipped past the curtains. I would read the paper. It was poetic justice. The paper woke me, so instead of taking my usual cursory glance at the headlines, I would read every story in the paper, and then I could eat, watch television, and take another pill. Full of purpose, I climbed out of bed.

I almost gave up. More Watergate fallout. Another stabbing at San Quentin. A group of "displaced homemakers" was petitioning Congress for reform of the marriage laws. Fifteen minutes had passed. Basic Development Corporation, low bidder on the project, had submitted final plans for the proposed Golden State Center to Richard Longstreet, San Francisco redevelopment director. That was too much. It was hard enough putting Richard out of my mind without reading about him and his idiotic Redevelopment Agency in the papers. Grimly, I leafed through to the obituary page, possibly hoping to see his name.

The name I saw wasn't Richard Longstreet, but Larry Hawkins. It was a short, uninformative article headed LOCAL EDITOR DIES IN FALL. I read it three times without stopping:

Larry Hawkins, 35, editor-publisher of the *People's Times*, a weekly newspaper devoted to local politics, was found dead this morning in an alley outside the *Times* offices at 1140 Cleveland Street, a police spokesman said. Hawkins, an apparent suicide, had fallen from his office window on the building's seventh floor. A note was found, the spokesman said.

Hawkins, self-styled "gadfly" of the City's political establishment, was a well-known local figure. The *People's Times* began publication three years ago. Hawkins is survived by his wife, Susanna, and two sons.

I put the paper down. So Larry Hawkins had committed suicide. I must have seen him a hundred times, maybe more—a slender man about five feet four, with a Byronic profile and a tumbling, unkempt headful of black curls, a rather attractive air of grubbiness about him. Although he was known to feel that anyone connected with City Hall was a natural adversary, there were people who considered it chic to flaunt their liberal tendencies and hound's-tooth cleanliness by inviting him to their parties. Perhaps they wanted to show they weren't afraid to let a righteous radical journalist loose in their china closets, no matter how out of place he might look and be.

Why he attended these gatherings I don't know, unless he was in search of stories. I doubt that was the only reason. I think he got some sort of thrill from swaggering into an impeccably dressed group wearing his dirty beige corduroy jacket, his patched jeans, and his cracked boots. His moral superiority was evident always. He showed it in his contempt for all of us, the establishment he despised and excoriated week after week in the *Times*. After a perfunctory handshake for his hostess, he would usually station himself as close to the food and drink as possible, watching everyone with quick, dark eyes. And the next week, likely as not, one of his fellow guests would turn up in the pages of the *Times* as having given the City rest-room contract to a toilet-paper firm owned by his brother-in-law.

I wasn't thinking about Larry now, but Richard. When I closed my eyes, I could see his long fingers curving around the telephone receiver, see his straight, navy blue, impeccably tailored back. I could hear his voice saying, impatiently, "Sure, I agree Larry Hawkins is a pain in the ass. . . ." I had stood in the doorway of the study, wearing the same salmon-colored peignoir I was wearing now. It was the end of October, and Richard was going to leave me.

Richard was nothing if not civilized, so he had waited until after I had my first cup of coffee, and told me over the raisin toast as we sat at the kitchen table having breakfast. Picking up crumbs and rolling them between his fingers, he broke out phrases like "better for both of us," and "well taken care of," and "haven't communicated in years."

There wasn't a word about his law student lady friend. I truly don't remember the occasion very well, even now.

Once he said, "Can't you understand, Maggie?" and reached out to touch my arm. I pulled back as if he had scalded me and knocked a jar of quince preserves off the table. Typical of Richard, to let other people make his messes for him while he watched, bemused at their clumsiness. As well as I remember, I hadn't said a word up until then, except a polite "You are?" when he said he was going. After the preserves jar broke, it seemed extremely important that it be cleaned up thoroughly and immediately. While I got up for paper towels, the phone rang.

There's an extension in the kitchen, but Richard said, vehemently, "God damn it to hell" and went to answer it in the study—glad, no doubt, to escape the sight of me bending pathetically over the preserves. When the floor was clean, I looked around for him. I must have been in shock, because I had forgotten about the phone call, and when I didn't see him it occurred to me that perhaps, having informed me of his intentions, he had simply left, not feeling the need for further elucidation. Dazed, I wandered into the living room and heard his voice coming from the study. I stood in the study door and saw Richard standing next to the desk, his back to me. His voice was irritated, emphatic. He said, "Sure, I agree Larry Hawkins is a pain in the ass. But you can absolutely take my word for it, we won't have to worry about him much longer." I turned around and walked back to the kitchen.

Now, I picked up the paper and read Larry's obituary one more time. We won't have to worry about him much longer. No. We certainly won't.

TWO

I didn't let myself think about it any longer, as if I had looked straight at the sun and didn't want to look again. I followed the rest of my daily routine carefully. Because I was still a little ahead of time, the evening pill had made me sleepy enough that I could reasonably switch off the television before the eleven-o'clock news, thus avoiding possible reminders of Larry's fate.

I moved through the next day like the zombie I was. It wasn't until slightly more than twenty-four hours after I had first read it that I walked back out on the sun porch and saw the previous day's paper, turned to Larry's obituary, lying beside my chair. I was overwhelmed by a rage so intense that I had to sit down before my knees gave way.

Larry and I had been in the same boat, hadn't we? Both of us had given Richard Longstreet a pain in the ass, and look at us now. Giving Richard a pain in the ass was obviously hazardous to your health, if not dangerous to your life.

In that bright burst of hatred I never doubted that Richard had somehow maneuvered Larry Hawkins into committing suicide, if he hadn't literally pushed him out the window. How else could he have been so certain on the telephone? "You can absolutely take my word for it," he had said. I remembered it more clearly than anything else that had happened that morning.

All at once, I couldn't sit still. Invigorated by anger, I got up and paced the room, clenching and unclenching my fists. It was so unfair. It was utterly, completely unfair. Things always went Richard's way. Does a newspaper editor bother you? A few months later he's dead. Does your wife cramp your style? Kick her aside. Don't under any circumstances let anything slow you down.

It would be such a satisfaction, just this once, to see him fail to get away with it. It would be the purest joy I could ever know to see him get caught. I stopped walking. It was impossible. There was nothing whatsoever I could do. Nothing. I sat down.

I thought about Larry. I had had only a single real conversation with him, and that took place because we were both somewhat drunk. It was at a fund-raising dinner for a Board of Supervisors candidate, held in a private room at one of the fancy Nob Hill hotels. Because of the terrible pressure of public service, the guest of honor hadn't shown up yet, and it was getting on for nine-thirty. The hors d'oeuvres trays were ravaged, and since dinner couldn't be served there was little to do but drink, or put one's head in an ashtray and go to sleep, or both. Richard was, as usual, deep in a huddle with the few selected bigwigs who could do him the most good, and I had exhausted my small talk. A white wine or even, God help us, some sort of mineral water would have been the trendy tipple, but I decided to continue bucking the trend and went to order another Scotch. Larry Hawkins was leaning up against the bar, his corduroy elbow just missing a puddle, and as I picked up my drink I noticed him watching me. He lifted his glass in a mocking little toast and then leaned over and said, "Bunch of turkeys."

"What?" I said.

He waved his glass, indicating the room, its inhabitants, and part of the ceiling. "Bunch of turkeys, man. Real bunch of turkeys."

I wasn't sure if he was insulting the crowd or announcing the menu. "Who is?"

His eyes narrowed. "Who is what?"

"A bunch of turkeys."

He looked at me glumly and turned away to his drink. "Aw, Christ, it's hopeless."

I wasn't to be put off. "Don't say it's hopeless. Just tell me."

"Can't you even *see*?" he said with exasperation. "Whole goddam room is full of goddam City Hall turkeys."

I sipped my drink. He pointed his index finger at me. The nail was chewed to the quick. "You look like an intelligent lady. What the hell are you doing here?"

"I'm married to one of the turkeys."

He looked sincerely sad. "Jeez," he said in a tone of regret. "Which one?"

"Richard Longstreet."

"Oh, *no*." His voice was a plaintive moan. "Not Redevelopment. God, I don't believe it."

At the time, I didn't appreciate his sympathy. "Yeah. Redevelopment."

He leaned toward me, full of sincerity. "Lady, if you want to take my advice you'll stay away from that Redevelopment bunch. I mean, I'm not kidding with you on that one. They're bad news." He nodded firmly.

"Thanks for telling me," I said. "It only comes about twenty years too late." I took my drink and wavered away from the bar.

Larry had said Redevelopment people were bad news, and he had been right. Now Larry had smashed himself on an alley pavement. That brash little man a suicide? Week after week, he had gone after City Hall corruption, buliding-code violations, consumer fraud, police department drinking, always with a strident assurance that left no room for self-doubt. Wasn't self-doubt a requirement for suicide?

You didn't know Larry, and you don't know the first thing about it, I chided myself. Wearily, I went to the kitchen to make a cheese sandwich. The bread was slightly stale. As I spread it with mayonnaise, I argued internally. I had heard

Richard promise someone that soon Larry wouldn't bother them again. Richard didn't know that I had heard him, and I was the only one who had heard him, besides the person at the other end of the line. That was point one.

Slicing the cheese, I went on to point two. If Larry was bothering Richard, it was probably because Richard was doing something Larry was planning to expose. I wanted to know what. Had the urbane, unflappable Richard Long-street made a misstep? Imagining his doing something wrong was easy. I had known for a long time that he was ruthless where his career was concerned. As a poor boy with the manners and tastes of the rich, he had of necessity hardened himself, left some of the virtues behind as excess baggage. Imagining his getting caught doing a wrong act was much more difficult. Richard was clever, and he liked to look good.

I had forgotten to make tea. The kettle would boil in a minute. The truth is, you want revenge, I told myself. There. There it was. I was angry, hurt, bitter, and now I had something that had never before been given to me—a weapon. Furthermore, if Richard *had* done something, something that led to Larry's death, wouldn't it be only the right thing to do, the moral thing to do, to find out what it was? To bring about justice? Justice for Larry and justice for me, all in one stroke?

My head was beginning to ache. Bring about justice. Maybe I thought I was Saint George, riding to kill the dragon and rescue the maiden in distress. Whereas actually I was the maiden—make that matron—in distress. In other words, helpless. I ate my sandwich and drank my tea and continued to sit staring at the squeezed-out tea bag in my saucer.

Larry might have been working on a story about Richard and the Redevelopment Agency at the time of his death. If he had been, it would mean—it wouldn't mean anything. But it *might* mean Richard had done something to Larry. It might. It might mean Richard was as mean a son of a bitch as I thought he was. I'd feel a lot of satisfaction in having my opinion confirmed.

Satisfaction was something I hadn't had much of lately, and the thought of feeling it again made my head reel faster than any pill ever could. All I really needed to know was what stories Larry had been working on before he went out the window. Suppose I could find out?

I couldn't find out. No way. I wasn't Saint George. I was just an ex-political wife, or a political ex-wife. Confined, more or less, to my really rather lovely home.

Well, hell. I could go to the *People's Times* and *ask*.

I could ask. What harm would it do? They could always tell me to get lost if they didn't want to say. If having somebody tell me to get lost would kill me, I'd have died after Richard Longstreet said it.

I must be nuts. Time for a pill.

I could ask. It wouldn't hurt anything. If I failed, so what? Failure was the story of my life. If I found out Larry had been investigating Richard—well, then I'd know.

Time for a pill.

I cleared away the dishes and sat down for an evening of television.

THREE

The *People's Times* was located in a grimy, dark-red-brick converted warehouse in the shadow of the freeway. Cleveland Street, in the industrial district south of Market Street, was hardly a street at all, but a litter-strewn passage where cars parked with two wheels on the crumbling sidewalks.

Although the geographical distance wasn't great, the atmosphere was completely different from the never-never land north of Market, where legions of visitors regularly left their hearts and discretionary dollars at the garish attractions of Fisherman's Wharf or Chinatown. Surely nobody wearing white shoes—footgear religiously shunned by true San Franciscans, thus the dead giveaway of a tourist—had ever walked down Cleveland Street.

Was *I* going to walk down Cleveland Street? My salmon-colored peignoir was hanging on a hook on the bathroom door. I was wearing a blue pantsuit, and my hair was brushed. I had managed to get the car started, drive all the way down here, and park in a vacant lot next to a dented yellow Volkswagen with a BOYCOTT GALLO sticker on the rear bumper. Now I was staring across at the building I had planned to enter, all the while clinging to the steering wheel as if it were a life ring somebody had thrown to me just before I went down for the third time. On the next street over, trucks roared by on their way to the freeway, adding their fumes to the haze that hung over the morning.

Making the gesture to get this far was something already. I could go back home now and feel that I had accomplished the seemingly insurmountable task of getting out of the house. That I should also get out of the car was too much to expect for one day.

To my surprise, I did get out of the car. Standing among broken glass, twisted cigarette packages, and weeds, I continued to stare at the building. The windows were blank and dusty, the dreariness of the façade relieved occasionally by a lopsided fern or an Indian-print bedspread hanging in a window. From somewhere not far away a jackhammer duplicated the pulses I felt in my head.

I was going in. If I weren't going in, I wouldn't have gone to the trouble to get dressed, make up a cover story, and unearth the two-year-old notebook—half full of calculus problems from my daughter Candace's high school days—that I was nervously clutching. I crossed the street.

At close range, the building was even seedier. The outer door listed on its hinges, opening into a foyer that smelled faintly of urine. On a yellowing piece of paper taped to the wall beside the elevator was a heavily amended list of tenants. Coalition for Justice and Equality, Gay Citizens League, Abolish Shock Therapy Now, *People's Times*. Seventh floor. I wasn't sure I liked the looks of the elevator, but when I entered and pressed the button the door creaked closed and it rumbled obediently, if slowly, upward.

When the door creaked open again, I stepped out into a musty-smelling hallway illuminated by milky light from a pebbled-glass window at the end. A few yards down on my left a door stood open and a phone was ringing. Next to the door, someone had written *People's Times* on the wall in red magic marker. I could still go back. The elevator hadn't even left yet. But at that moment it began to reverberate, and I stepped into the reception office of the *People's Times*.

My first impression was of paper. All sorts of paper. Tied, piled-up bundles of *Times*es along one wall. On the battered wooden desk in front of me stacks, or drifts, of magazines and opened mail, some of which had found a less crowded resting place on the floor. A threadbare green couch was littered with the daily newspapers, and pigeon-holes on the wall behind the desk were overflowing with envelopes and flyers. The room was empty, and the phone was still ringing.

As I stood uncertainly, a girl with a large halo of frizzy red hair burst into the room, screamed "*Screw* that phone!" grabbed the receiver, surveyed me, and said, crisply, "*Times*."

She held up a finger to indicate she'd be through in a minute. Her exuberant hair, big blue eyes, and freckles cried out for an oversized polka-dot bow tie and a bright yellow derby, but instead she wore the top to a set of long underwear, bib overalls, and hiking boots. "Yeah, we plan to keep publishing. Andrew Baffrey's taking over as editor," she said, sitting down at the desk and resting one leg on the piles of mail, knocking a few more pieces to the ground.

As she listened, she picked up a letter, squinted at it, tossed it aside. Then she rolled her eyes exaggeratedly. "No, I think Andrew will do a great job, and I'm sure he'll want to use the story you wrote, but we're in a little bit of a mess right now. Could you maybe call back next week? Thanks a lot."

Putting down the phone, she looked at me and said, "Writers are incredible. What can I do for you?"

Sweat from my palms had made my notebook feel slippery. "I'm Maggie Wilson," I said. It was my maiden name. I'd decided to leave "Longstreet" out of it.

The girl offered a hand which was even more freckled than her face. "Betsy O'Shea."

Larry Hawkins's death didn't seem to have fazed Betsy O'Shea, but apparently she was a type it would take a lot to faze. Of all the attitudes I had imagined I might find at the *People's Times*, this brisk friendliness was probably the last I had expected. Encouraged, I launched into my cover story. "I'm a journalism student at State. I'm in the reentry program there, you know, training older women for the job market. . . ."

Betsy looked interested. "My landlady went through that about a year ago. She said it was great." She shrugged. "We don't have any jobs right now, though. See, you may not have heard, but our editor—"

"I know, I know," I interrupted. "I'm not here about a job. It's for a class assignment. I want to do a story on Larry Hawkins."

The blue eyes glazed. "You and a dozen other people."

Oh God. I was losing her goodwill already. I stumbled on. "I guess it isn't a very original idea, but I thought I might be able to give it a new slant."

"How many times have I heard that one? No offense." She rubbed her temples. "Reentry program, huh? Did your old man run out on you? If you don't mind my asking."

15

My face burned. What a fool I was, coming here to expose myself to this strange girl's casual curiosity instead of staying up on Lake Street where I belonged. "I guess that's right."

I caught a shade of pity on her face. "That's what happened to my landlady." She waved a hand at the couch. "Sit down for a minute, why don't you?"

As I crossed to the couch, the phone rang again and she yelled, "Kit, catch the phones for a while, OK?" I moved some newspapers and sat down.

"What kind of story did you have in mind?" she asked.

My plan was to start slowly and back into the big question. "I'd like to do an account of his last day, interspersed with history about the *Times*, stories he's done, things like that. Sort of a montage." Actually, I thought, the idea wasn't half bad.

"His last day, huh?" Betsy leaned back and looked at the ceiling. "That would be two days ago. It was a fairly typical day around here."

"It was?" I opened my notebook.

"Yeah. Which means it was frantic from beginning to end. Let's see. Larry came in around noon and was his normal self, ranting at everybody. That afternoon was the thing with September Apple."

"September Apple?"

"A person. She was really into ecology at one point, so she took that name. Her real name is something like Mary."

"She came in that afternoon?"

"She was always coming in. Larry gave her an assignment. Like everybody else in this town, she wants to be a writer. He finally told her to do something about poetry. Andrew Baffrey had been pushing him to use artsy stuff occasionally. So she worked and worked, and she was around here a lot. This place is the biggest outpatient clinic in San Francisco." Betsy glanced around as if she wouldn't be surprised to see outpatients emerging from the walls.

"Did the story get published?"

"Are you kidding? That's what all the shrieking was about. She came in that afternoon, the day after she'd turned it in, and God, what a fight she and Larry had. I mean, the door of his office was closed, but I could hear their voices all the way out here. Finally, she came flying out of there just about hysterical and took off and I haven't seen her since. You have to understand that wasn't particularly unusual, though. Larry had that effect on writers."

I was scratching away in the notebook, getting it all down. I didn't want to blow my cover by not looking interested. "They were fighting about the story?"

"Probably. See"—Betsy leaned forward—"don't put this in your article, but constructive criticism wasn't in Larry's vocabulary. You either wrote it his way or screw you. He was always sure he was one hundred percent right."

"Did anything happen after that?"

"Not much. Larry spent a long time in his office with Andrew Baffrey that afternoon. They must have been in there three hours, and then Andrew left, and *man*." Betsy was silent for a moment, thoughtful. "I tell you, Larry came out to get a cup of coffee, and he was shaking like a leaf. It was strange, you know?" The sadness I had missed earlier washed over her face. Her fingers twisted a frizzy tendril of hair.

"He wasn't usually the nervous type?" Pretty soon, the intrepid reentry reporter was going to slip in the jackpot question.

Betsy chuckled mournfully. "How could he run a paper like the *Times* and be nervous, with people threatening to sue him all the time? I feel bad about it now. I saw he was upset. Maybe if I'd said something, it would've made a difference, and he wouldn't . . ." She sighed. "So. He went back into his office, closed the door, and nobody saw him until his body was found by the garbagemen. Is that all you need?"

The moment had come. "Just one more thing. I was

wondering—" I began, just as a flabby blond man appeared in the doorway.

I heard Betsy mutter "Oh, no" as he walked unsteadily toward her. His hair, a razor cut grown too long, looked greasy. His belly hung over the pants of his ghastly brushed denim leisure suit. He rested his knuckles on the desk and leaned toward her.

"Well." He managed to convey hostility in the single syllable.

"Hi, Ken," said Betsy calmly.

"So Hawkins has gone to his reward." The man had a resonant, theatrical voice. I almost thought I had heard it before. His face, with its straight, fleshy nose and prominent chin, looked familiar, too. Was he an actor? I flashed through the productions I'd seen by the local repertory company, but couldn't fit him into any role.

"That's right."

"Who's in charge now?" His belligerence was deepening.

"Andrew Baffrey."

"He in?"

Betsy shook her head. "Sorry. He's gone out for a while."

The man leaned heavily across the desk and gripped Betsy's shoulder. Her expression didn't change. "You sure he's not around?"

"Absolutely." Betsy slid away from his grasp.

The man staggered, righted himself, and gazed blearily around. He wandered toward me and sank down on the other end of the couch. I could smell the liquor now. His eyes slid over me without interest, and I was again positive I knew him. "Baffrey, huh?" he said.

"Right. But he isn't in."

"Is he as big a son of a bitch as Hawkins? Or is he a human being?"

"Andrew's OK."

He leaned forward in a parody of earnestness. "Look,

18

hon. Now that Larry's gone, don't you think this rag could print a retraction? I mean, enough's enough."

Betsy shook her head. "You won't get anywhere with that, Ken. The story was true and we could prove it. Like Larry told you, the issue is closed."

"The issue is closed," he mimicked. "Shit. Larry Hawkins thinks it's all right to take away a man's job for the sake of a story? What kind of screwed-up values are those?"

Now I knew who he was. Kenneth MacDonald, Channel 8's local-news attempt to duplicate Eric Sevareid. He had been the picture of rock-solid propriety, narrating three-alarm fires, murders in the Tenderloin, drug busts in Berkeley, the new gorilla at the zoo, and the mayor's birthday party all with the same sonorous pomposity. He'd had an editorial segment—"The View from Here," or something like that—in which he'd strung together platitudes on subjects of local interest.

I goggled at him. He'd been ruggedly handsome, with features worthy of Mount Rushmore. Now, his face was puffy, bloated, his eyes insignificant in the surrounding flesh. I remembered that I hadn't seen him on Channel 8 lately.

"I'll tell you again," Ken was saying. "I told Larry, and I'll tell you, and I'll tell this Andrew character that I didn't know who owned that place. It was just a two-bedroom cabin at Tahoe, not a palace, for Chrissakes."

"I think Larry's point was that people in your position have to be careful," Betsy said.

"You do? Well, I think Larry's point was to sell a few more copies of his miserable paper, and he didn't care whose ass he had to trample to do it." Ken got laboriously to his feet. "It's no wonder the little rat bastard killed himself. He probably realized what a creep he really was." He shoved his chest forward, fists clenched at his sides.

Betsy didn't respond. Under her steady gaze, his stance gradually lost its antagonism. When he next spoke, it was with more bravado than conviction. "I'll be back. I'm going to talk to Baffrey about that retraction. You haven't seen the last of me."

"Sure," Betsy said. "Just give us a couple of days to get on our feet, OK?"

"Right," he said, apparently mollified. For the first time, it came to his attention that I was in the room. He looked at me with an inquiring stare.

"That's Maggie Wilson," Betsy said.

The change in him was instantaneous. Meeting a member of the public, he was the superstar television commentator once more. He flashed me a grin that had once been photogenic and held out his hand. "Kenneth MacDonald, Channel Eight. Pleased to meet you," he said heartily. Before I could reply he dropped my hand and meandered from the room.

Once he made it out the door Betsy turned to me. "Sorry about that."

"I see what you mean about the outpatient clinic."

"You don't know the half. Poor Ken. He was way too much of a lightweight to hold his own with Larry." She folded an airplane from one of the papers on her desk and sailed it toward the window, where it crashed against the glass. "What a drag, right? Was there anything else you needed for your story?"

At last. I pretended to think for a moment. "The only other thing is, I thought it might add depth if I could say which stories Larry was working on at the time of his death. Give the feeling that his work must continue, and so on."

Betsy shook her head. "It's not a bad idea, but you're talking to the wrong person. Larry played close to the chest. Totally. It could be that nobody knew, because that's the way he was. If anybody had an idea, it would be Andrew Baffrey, and he's gone out."

I wilted. I had dragged myself down here, skipped my morning pill, sat through a tirade by a drunken former television commentator, only to run full tilt against failure.

"Would he be willing to talk with me?" I could hear the tightness in my voice.

"I doubt it," Betsy said slowly. "He's taking over the paper, and he's also very upset about Larry's death. He's going to have a lot on his mind."

I told myself I had known this wasn't going to work out, that it had been stupid ever to think it would. Ever to think anything would. I closed my notebook and stood up, leaden with disappointment. "Thanks anyway."

Betsy looked at me. "You've *got* to have that one detail?"

"I just—just thought it would add the right finishing touch. I'd planned it that way, and I sort of described it to my professor . . ." My voice was heading into the upper registers. I prayed it wouldn't actually crack as I gabbled through this pack of lies.

I could see the decision on Betsy's face before she said, "Oh rats. I've had enough emotional trauma in the past few days to last a lifetime. Come in tomorrow morning and I'll try to shoehorn you in to see Andrew for a few minutes."

The rush of relief I felt almost overwhelmed me. I gushed my thanks and she accepted them nonchalantly, cautioning me only to leave my phone number so she could reach me if she had to reschedule.

I was standing in the doorway thanking her once again when a woman pushed me aside to get into the room. Her long brown hair was windblown, her face a deep pink. She wore jeans, boots, and a heavy zip-fronted sweater with a pattern of gray llamas on it. She stood in the middle of the room and said, tremulously but carefully, enunciating each word, "Betsy, I cannot stand it any longer. People have *got* to get off my back. I cannot stand it—" She broke off and bowed her head. I heard her emit a little squeak.

Betsy was beside her in a second, putting an arm around her and leading her to the couch. Before they reached it, the woman was sobbing convulsively.

Whether or not Betsy had had enough emotional trauma,

she was obviously going to have more. She sat next to the woman, saying, "What happened, Susanna? Did somebody do something to you?" but the woman only wailed louder, her face clenched like a child's, stray hair clinging to the wetness of her cheeks and lips. Betsy said, "Maggie, there's a water cooler back in the newsroom. Bring a cup, would you?"

Susanna? Susanna Hawkins, Larry's widow. Heading in the direction Betsy had indicated, I began the search for the water cooler.

FOUR

Newsroom seemed an extravagant term to apply to the collection of ramshackle desks, jerry-built tables, and dented filing cabinets I found down a short hall. The typewriters looked ancient enough to have been used for the on-the-scene reports from the '06 quake. The atmosphere was subdued. A few of the desks were occupied by people reading or staring into space. Two men and a woman, all dressed in post-hippie style—much the same as hippie style, but without fringe or beads—were clustered around a filing cabinet, speaking in low tones. They glanced at me, their young, worried faces registering the fact that I looked expensively out of place, then turned back to their conversation. Here, the pall left by Larry's death was tangible.

I spotted the water cooler in a corner, and filled a paper cup. "I don't know," a ponytailed young man in the filing-cabinet group was saying. "The way Andrew's freaking out there's no telling what's going to happen."

"He'll pull himself together. Give him half a chance," the woman said, sounding unconvinced.

"I don't know," the man said again, and they fell silent.

When I returned to the outer office, Susanna's sobs had reached the gasping, hiccuping stage. Betsy was still sitting beside her, patting her back, and when she saw me she said "Thanks" and took the cup.

Susanna's face was more composed now, and I saw for the first time how lovely she was. Even brimming with tears, her eyes were a stunning violet blue, and her flushed skin seemed almost translucent. She didn't look older than twenty-three or twenty-four, at least ten years younger than Larry had been. She watched me over the rim of the cup, and when she had drunk she said, "Who are you?"

"This is Maggie Wilson," Betsy said. "She's a journalism student. She's going to write a story about Larry."

The eyes I had been admiring animated instantly with dislike. "Oh, fabulous," Susanna said. "Fantastic. I've made my entrance in full view of a reporter. I can't believe it."

"I'm not really a reporter—" I began, but she cut me off.

"I *said* people have to get off my back," she snapped fretfully. "Can't I even walk in here without a thousand hassles?"

Betsy made a protesting gesture. "Susanna, Maggie isn't—"

"Look." Susanna got up and began to pace. "I went to the coroner's office, all right? And I got a million stupid questions, and sign this and sign that before they'll give me Larry's things. And then—then downstairs I get accosted by this *idiot*, this pimply-faced kid who said he *worshiped* Larry and wants to write some kind of memorial."

I was obviously in the wrong place. Susanna Hawkins was in no mood to put up with prying journalists, and that's what she thought I was. I edged toward the door.

"He wanted to know all this stuff," Susanna rushed on. "Why did I think Mr. Hawkins did it? Didn't I think he was

23

a martyr, some kind of *saint*?" She giggled breathlessly. "And do you know what he wanted then?" She was looking at me, talking to me. "He wanted to see the note Larry left. Can you believe it? He said he'd consider it a privilege. You know what I should have done?" Her voice was rising. She went to the couch and fumbled in her handbag, pulling out a small piece of white paper. "I should have said, 'Sure, kid. Take it. *Read* it. It's *yours*!'"

She flung the paper in my direction and turned around, sobbing once again, Betsy at her side. The paper made a couple of lazy loops and settled on the floor. I should leave it there, I told myself. I glanced at it. The writing was facing up. I heard inquiring voices. Susanna's hysterics had aroused the newsroom. I picked up the paper. The note was short, written with a black felt-tipped pen. There was no salutation, and the writing was angular and positive: "Sorry to do this to you and the kids, but believe me, there's no other way. Forgive me, baby." The signature, a flourishing "Larry," took up half the sheet.

As I placed the note on the couch next to Susanna's handbag, the newsroom's inhabitants crowded in, asking what was going on. I walked out the door, down the hall, and leaned gratefully on the elevator button.

I sat in the car trying to catch my breath. My visit to the *Times* had proved considerably more exciting than a two-Campari-and-soda lunch and a charity fashion show. I must be exhausted, ready to go home and catch a nap.

Reluctantly, I started the car. Sure. Mission accomplished for one day. Got to rest up for my encounter with Andrew Baffrey tomorrow. As I drove slowly out of the vacant lot, I realized that I was hungry. Although it was still a bit early, it could be reasonably construed as lunch time, and of course it made no sense at all to go home until after I'd had some lunch.

I wasn't in the mood, though, to go to any of my former haunts, where I might be pitied and patronized, either by headwaiters or acquaintances who would gossip about

Richard or urge me to take up Japanese flower arranging or primal scream therapy.

I drove aimlessly around the neighborhood until I spotted a diner advertising CHINESE AMERICAN CUISINE and BREAKFAST ALL DAY. Sitting at the counter, I ordered pancakes, sausages, and coffee and eavesdropped on three khaki-clad men sitting a few stools down who were drinking coffee and arguing about what should be done to improve Candlestick Park. By the time they agreed that the goddam thing should be bulldozed, I had devoured my food and was feeling surprisingly content.

I hadn't found out what I wanted to know at the *Times*, true. Still, I couldn't help thinking the visit had been, in some sense, a success. Despite Susanna Hawkins's frenzy, despite the unpleasantness of Ken MacDonald—or perhaps even because of those things—it had been a fascinating window into something new.

On the other hand, I told myself, I can't get distracted by side issues. If I don't find out what Richard's connection with Larry was, the whole thing will be meaningless. Don't lose sight of the main question.

As I paid the bill, it occurred to me that Richard had hardly entered my consciousness at all during the time I'd spent at the *Times*. He had receded to a mathematical abstraction, a term I wanted to try in an equation. But now here he was, fully fleshed in my mind, where he had been awaiting his chance to grasp me again. As I walked down the gusty sidewalk, grit blowing in my eyes, I realized that I should have known he'd still be lurking there, that he wouldn't go away and leave me in peace.

Behind the wheel, I found myself still unwilling to go home. Now that I was out, it was almost as difficult to return as it had been to emerge. I drove, looking at the drab buildings, the trucks unloading, the newspapers blowing across the street, until it occurred to me that I was only a few blocks from the Civic Center, and the main branch of the public library. I could read some back issues of the

Times. Richard had changed his subscription to his love nest on Russian Hill, and I hadn't been particularly interested in city politics lately, my ignorance of Ken MacDonald's problems proof of my inattention. Relieved to have a destination once again, I drove to the Civic Center and parked in the underground garage.

In fifteen minutes, I was sinking into the somnolent atmosphere of the library's newspaper reading room, the past six months' *Times*es in a stack in front of me. The only sounds were the crackling of newsprint, the occasional clicking of a microfilm machine, and the soft, purring snore of the grizzled old man sitting at the end of my table, the *Christian Science Monitor* open in front of him and his hands folded on his chest.

I looked at the *Times*es. Twenty-five cents a copy. An untidy, dog-eared heap of newsprint representing Larry Hawkins's life's work. Larry hadn't had much talent for design. The paper was the size of an advertising throwaway. The headline of the top issue trumpeted, MAYOR FUDGES ON DRUG REHAB PROGRAM. I picked it up and began to read.

After an hour, I was almost numb from the barrage of accusatory prose. Larry's sources had been numerous, his fund of anger apparently inexhaustible. His own byline appeared most frequently, but there were also stories by Andrew Baffrey, managing editor, in almost every issue. Baffrey, it seemed to me, was a more balanced reporter, his prose considerably less rabble-rousing than Larry's and occasionally even humorous, humor being a sin Larry never committed.

Turning a page, I found myself staring into the stalwart gaze of a promotional photograph of Ken MacDonald. His jawline was as square as I remembered it, his mouth as confident. The picture was captioned, "Channel 8 sooth-sayer Kenneth MacDonald. What was he doing at Tahoe at a developer's expense?"

The story was brief, the facts tightly nailed down. Ken had spent two weeks in a Lake Tahoe cabin which Larry's checking had revealed to be owned by Jane Malone, executive vice president of Basic Development Corporation. Several weeks after his return, Ken had delivered an impassioned editorial in favor of the Golden State Center, one of Basic's key projects, a high-rise development near the waterfront that had been anathema to San Francisco's environmentalists. When questioned, he had claimed the cabin had been offered to him by a friend, and he hadn't known who the actual owner was.

"The citizens of San Francisco aren't being given the news on Channel 8, they're hearing the gospel according to the high rise," Larry had written. "Now we know why. It's the old story of one hand washing the other. We think, however, these revelations of his compromised objectivity should wash so-called 'reporter' Kenneth MacDonald right off the screen." Two weeks later, in a column headed "Follow-Up," Larry wrote, "Kudos to Channel 8 management for their prompt dumping of developers' darling Kenneth MacDonald, who spent a vacation in a cabin owned by Basic Development and then came out foursquare behind Basic's pet project, the Golden State Center (*Times*, Nov. 29)."

There went Ken down the tubes. I looked through the rest of the papers, but found nothing further to interest me. While the Redevelopment Agency, and Richard as its director, had come in for a fair share of knocks and snide remarks, there had been no major exposé. If there had been a strong connection between Richard and Larry, no intimation of it had crept into print. Yawning, I folded the last issue and handed the stack to the librarian. At last, I was ready to go home.

FIVE

When I arrived the next morning, the *Times* office showed signs of casting off the stagnation of the day before. Several scruffy-looking people, presumably staff members, were milling around in Betsy's office reading mail or the morning paper, talking and drinking coffee. Betsy sat behind her desk looking the same as before, except today she was wearing a purple leotard with her overalls. When she saw me, she smiled.

"I thought you might not come back at all after yesterday," she said. "Susanna was really overwrought."

"She has reason to be upset."

"Yeah, but she was pretty hard on you. Only, it wasn't *you*, if you know what I mean." She got up. "I'll see if Andrew's free."

She was back shortly. "He only has a minute, but you can go in now. Straight through the newsroom, and it's the door right in front of you."

The newsroom was also more populated than yesterday, with people tapping at typewriters, dialing phones, and generally looking productive. Evidently, Andrew Baffrey had managed to marshal his troops. The door that must be his was closed. A piece of paper was taped to it on which was written, in blue pencil, *Editur at work*. I knocked, and a hoarse voice beckoned me in.

The office was the size of a broom closet. The young man standing at the window looked as if he hadn't slept in weeks. The part of his face that wasn't obscured by a brown beard was a pale, sickly yellow. His large brown eyes were red-rimmed and blurred with grief or exhaustion, and his hair stood away from his head as if he had spent a lot of time running his hands through it. He had the raw-boned body of a high-school basketball player who hasn't quite filled out yet. I judged him to be about twenty-five years old.

"Andrew Baffrey," he said. I told him I was Maggie Wilson, and we shook hands. He had the knobbiest wrists I had ever seen, or perhaps that impression came from the fact that his sweater sleeves were too short. His palm was clammy, and I could feel a tremor in his fingers. He gestured to a folding chair for me and sat down behind his desk. "Betsy says you want to do a story on Larry. What for?" he asked.

Accustomed to Betsy's friendly cooperation, I found the question brusque. Slightly off balance, I launched into my journalism-student story, hoping I sounded confident. The truth was, I had once thought about entering the program for real, so I knew a bit about it. Andrew made no comment, and I felt myself losing conviction under his noncommittal gaze. I finished, lamely, "I want to write about what Larry Hawkins did on his final day, and intersperse that with flashbacks about the history of the *Times*."

"I see." He drummed his fingers on the desk, watching them rise and fall. Finally, he looked back at me and said, "What do you want from me?"

I was getting thoroughly unnerved. "I thought it would add to my article if I knew what stories he was working on at the time of his death. I mean, help me understand his motives and so forth." I had never before realized how important the nods, smiles, and sympathetic sounds of normal conversation were. The silence was unbearable, so I chattered on. "The stories might provide clues to why he did it, I thought. From what I understand, suicide was very much out of character for him."

A jolt of pain crossed Andrew's face, gone almost before I had seen it, leaving his eyes a little redder than before.

29

"You could say that," he muttered. He stood up, slipping his fingers in the back pockets of his faded jeans, and wandered back to the window. "What was your name again?"

"Maggie Wilson."

He rested one foot on the windowsill, leaned his elbow on his knee, and looked at me. He was wearing a battered-looking pair of running shoes, their electric blue the brightest color in the room. "Maggie, I want to know why you're here," he said casually.

This was it. My face was getting hot. "I told you."

He shook his head. "I don't believe you." He didn't seem angry, or even particularly interested. "For one thing, I know the guy who runs that program at State. When he sends students over, he always calls me to see if it's OK. Should I give him a jingle to ask about you?"

Looking down at Candace's notebook in my lap, I shook my head. I must look like a whipped puppy. I wish to God I'd never heard of Andrew Baffrey.

He crossed the room and perched on the corner of his desk in front of me. "Then I want to know what you're doing," he said. "Did you come here for some weird kick, or are you snooping around for somebody?"

Mustering my dignity, I stood up. My nose began to prickle, a bad sign meaning I might cry. "I'll leave," I said, making a tentative movement toward the door.

Without getting up, Andrew caught me by the forearm. "I want to know what you're doing here," he repeated, his voice level.

I was an idiot, a fool, and now I looked like a fool in front of this loathsome, self-righteous apprentice muckraker. I pulled my arm away, searching frantically and vainly for another plausible lie.

"Surely you must realize how many people would like to know what Larry Hawkins was keeping under his hat," Andrew said. "Did you think you could walk in and ask and I'd tell you, just like that? How long do you think the *Times* would last if we went around discussing our stories before they appeared in the paper? I want to know what your interest is, Maggie. That's all."

His eyes seemed dark and huge. Through the dizziness of my embarrassment I grasped that I had taken a risk and I had gotten caught, fair and square. Without realizing I was about to do it, I said, "My name is Maggie Longstreet."

I couldn't tell if it meant anything to him. He nodded and said, "Fine. Let's go have a cup of coffee while we talk about the rest."

Once we were out on the street, Andrew's color looked better, and as we walked he began to swing his arms. Watching him, it occurred to me that his usual temperament could be quite different from the anxiety-ridden side of him I had seen so far. Unaccountably, I felt my own spirits rise, and I took a deep breath of factory effluvia.

"This place I'm taking you to has terrible Danish, and the coffee is even worse," he said.

I was grateful for his effort to put me at ease. "What a recommendation."

"It's my favorite place to hang out, because it has flamingos painted on the walls."

Not only flamingos, but red and pink hibiscus, assorted palm trees, and an aquamarine lagoon, all somewhat chipped and faded, adorned one wall of the Tropicana Cafeteria. The mural's vegetation was supplemented by a lush assortment of plastic foliage. Andrew seated me next to a particularly bushy (and dusty) specimen and went to the counter, returning in a few minutes with coffees and Danish. Putting mine in front of me he said, "Sink your teeth into this, if at all possible." Sitting across the table, he leaned back to look at the flamingos for a moment. When he turned to me, the lines of tension had returned to his face.

"It might help if I tell you I know who you are," he said. "I've been poking around picking up gossip in the city departments for several years now. I know who Richard

Longstreet is, and I know you've just gotten a divorce, or dissolution, or whatever. Do you want to take it from there?"

Andrew had been right about the Danish. It was hard to chew, and even harder to swallow. I choked down a bite with the aid of some coffee. "I wanted to find out if Larry had been working on any stories relating to Richard."

He didn't seem surprised. "Why? Would that give you some leverage in the settlement, or something?"

"No, nothing like that." I sat silent for a moment. My idea that Richard had somehow been involved in Larry's death now seemed irrational, the unhinged fantasy of a vindictive, disappointed woman. "I thought . . ." I cleared my throat and started over. "I thought it would help me understand things a little better. The kind of person Richard was, I mean."

"Um." Andrew's face was shaded by his bony fingers, but he was watching me closely. "There's one thing that puzzles me."

"What?"

"How did you get the idea that Larry might have been investigating Richard? When Larry was on to something, he told absolutely nobody, not even me. He might let me in on it to the extent that he needed legwork, or he might drop a hint or two, but nobody got the full picture until it was ready to go in the paper."

"So you don't know whether Larry had anything on Richard or not?" From the strain I could feel around my eyes, I knew I was watching Andrew as intently as he was watching me.

"I didn't say that. I asked why you thought he did."

"I suppose maybe Richard mentioned it at some point." I could feel him willing me to go on, feel his knowledge that I wasn't being frank. I clamped my jaw, determined not to tell everything I knew unless he gave something too. We stared at each other. I felt as if he and I were in a magnetic field—a field enclosing us, our table, two cooling cups of coffee, two inedible Danish pastries.

Andrew broke the tension first. It evaporated at the first sign of his grin. "I'll settle for a draw on that round," he said. "Why don't we have some fresh coffee?"

As he set the new, steaming cups beside the cold ones he said, "I've got a proposition for you, Maggie."

All at once I felt reckless. "Name it."

He took a large bite of his Danish and chewed thoughtfully, leaving a few crumbs clinging to his beard. Then, ticking his points off on his fingers, he said, "I know something you want to know. You know something I want to know. Now this is the deal." He edged his chair closer and leaned conspiratorially across the table. "Why don't we tell each other what we want to know?"

I nearly laughed out loud. "They certainly teach you clever ways to elicit information in journalism school."

"I never went to journalism school. I was a political science major." He smiled. "What do you say?"

It was obviously the only way I'd find out anything more. "All right. But only if you go first."

"Do you know," he said ruminatively, "those are the exact words my first little girlfriend used when I asked her to play doctor. But if I had ever learned anything from experience, would I be where I am today?"

His face sobered. "Here goes. Larry was working on a story about the Redevelopment Agency, especially Richard Longstreet. Now, you're going to ask, what was the story about? I don't know. Like I said, Larry was paranoid about leaks, but at the same time if he was on something very large, he couldn't resist making tantalizing remarks about it. For the past several months, he's been telling me, 'We're going to get those Redevelopment bastards,' or 'I'm going to blow Richard Longstreet right off the map.' So the answer to your question is, yeah. Larry had a story, and it was big."

So I'd gotten my answer, after all the trouble. There was

a connection between Larry and Richard. I felt as if I had walked through a doorway and Andrew's words had slammed the door behind me. Now I was in a place I'd never been before, and there was no way to go back.

SIX

"You got pale. Are you OK?" Andrew said.

My face felt immobile, as if encased in plaster. I had trouble moving my lips to ask, "Is there any way of finding out more about the story?"

Looking at me closely, Andrew hesitated before he answered. "I'm not sure. I haven't been through Larry's office yet, his private papers. It could be there, or it could be that he was carrying the whole thing around in his head. Sometimes he worked that way." He sat back in his chair. "Your turn."

A bargain was a bargain. Besides, as I tried to think how to begin, my suspicions once again seemed to melt into absurdity. I knotted my hands together in my lap. "You're going to think I'm crazy."

"After three years at the *Times*, I consider craziness a purely relative concept."

"When I saw Larry's obituary in the paper, I remembered something I overheard Richard say about Larry on the telephone a couple of months ago."

"Oh yeah?"

"Yes. I don't know who he was talking to, but he told the person that he knew Larry Hawkins was a pain in the ass, but they wouldn't have to worry about him much longer.

When I remembered, I got curious and I wanted to find out—" I broke off. Find out what?

"Holy shit," said Andrew. He looked stunned. "You mean, like—you think Richard might have had something to do with Larry's death?"

I shrank from hearing it put so baldly. "Probably not," I said hastily. "Really it was just that I was curious. I said it was crazy."

"Not especially crazy." Andrew's face, so yellow and unhealthy-looking when I had met him earlier, now surged with color. I was surprised, thrown off balance by the intensity of his reaction. Surely he could see how tenuous the whole thing was, I assured myself. He wouldn't begin a campaign for Richard's arrest on the basis of a few words.

"Listen, this is strictly confidential," I said, wishing I'd said it earlier.

He nodded vigorously. "Sure, sure. It's just that this makes—" He dug a spiral-bound notebook from his breast pocket and shoved it across the table to me. "I owe you. In the next couple of days I'll know if Larry left behind anything on that story. Give me your number, and I'll call and tell you what I find out."

Writing down my name and number, I said, "I appreciate this. But you don't actually *owe* me anything."

He flipped the notebook shut and replaced it in his pocket. "Yes, I do. A hell of a lot more than you realize. You'll hear from me."

We walked the few blocks back to the *Times* in silence. I was trying to assimilate what Andrew had told me. Now I knew for sure that Richard had been in danger from Larry. An exposé, a scandal, his photograph in the papers—how he would despise it. I wondered what he had done, what Larry had been preparing to divulge. I would give a great deal to know. It might help me to assess, or reassess, the past twenty years. At my side Andrew was equally thoughtful, his head bent, his hands shoved in the pockets of his red nylon windbreaker.

When we reached Cleveland Street he shook my hand, promising once again to call me soon. I watched him lope into the building, then turned toward my car.

Driving back home I thought about Andrew, wondering if my daughter Candace, now a sophomore at Stanford, would like him. I doubted it. Candace had inherited too much of Richard's concern with appearances to be impressed by a threadbare crusading journalist. A budding stockbroker would be more in her line, or a young lawyer in a three-piece suit just starting out at one of the better Montgomery Street firms. Like father, like daughter.

Which was too bad, because it would be fun having somebody like Andrew Baffrey around. If he started seeing Candace, the two of them might come for dinner sometimes. He'd regale Candace and me with the latest political gossip, or tell stories about the crazy things that had happened at the paper. The three of us would sit around and laugh. . . .

I dragged my mind from this completely improbable scenario. Candace would never look at him twice, and he was probably taken anyway. A man as attractive as he was would have been snapped up long ago.

The phone was ringing when I got home. I heard it as I was closing the garage door. For reasons that were never adequately explained to me—something about the foundations? Reinforcement against the next big quake?—the renovation of our house left us with an attached garage but no inside access to it. That circumstance frequently made me wish the place had been leveled in 1906. Wishing it yet again, I sprinted up the front steps and caught the phone, miraculously, on the tenth ring. The female voice at the other end was unfamiliar.

"Maggie Wilson?"

"Yes?" Someone at the *Times*, since she thought my name was Wilson, but it didn't sound like Betsy.

"This is Susanna Hawkins."

I hoped my gasp of surprise was lost in my general

breathlessness, and hoped even more that Susanna hadn't called to finish the job of berating me she had started yesterday. "Yes, hello," I said warily.

Her voice was soft and a little nervous, a tone totally unlike that of our former encounter. "I got your number from Betsy O'Shea. I want to apologize for the way I acted yesterday. It was unforgivable, but I hope you understand—"

I rushed to reassure her. "Of course I do. Please don't worry about it."

"I'm really ashamed of myself, and I'd like to make it up to you," she went on. "I thought maybe I could help with your article, so I got together one of Larry's bios and some reprints of articles about the *Times*. I'm more or less"—she breathed deeply—"going through things anyway, and—" I heard a crash, a child wailing in the background, a dog barking. "Oh, God. Can you hang on a minute?" she said, and left the phone.

Listening to her chastise child and dog, I mused that this was a pretty kettle of fish. I was thoroughly ashamed that Susanna Hawkins, newly widowed, had taken the trouble to help me with an article that didn't exist. In fact, the effort at conciliation seemed a bit excessive on her part. Since I didn't want to risk causing another scene like the one at the *Times* office, it would be best to go along with her, take whatever she had for me, and slink away.

This decision coincided with her return to the telephone. "Sorry," she said. "I guess I was saying you could stop by if you wanted to and pick up that information."

I thanked her emphatically. She gave me an address in Bernal Heights and directions on how to get there. As I was replacing the receiver I heard another shriek in the background and mentally gave thanks that Candace was no younger than nineteen.

Unwilling to keep Susanna waiting and also wanting to get the whole thing over with, I started out immediately. Bernal Heights was exactly in the direction I'd just come from. As I drove south on Van Ness Avenue once again, past the opera house and the lavish automobile dealerships, it occurred to me that I'd spent more time south of Market in the past two days than I had in the previous two years. The traffic wasn't bad, and in twenty minutes or so I was parking on Barton Street, across the street from the number Susanna had given me.

Judging by the neighborhood, the *Times* hadn't made Larry wealthy. Barton Street, neither fashionable nor rich-hippie funky, was lined with modest, pastel-colored houses fronting on cracked sidewalks, straggling up the side of a steep hill. Now, at noon, the street was empty, except for two large dogs trotting purposefully toward the hilltop, but I could imagine that after school hours it would be alive with children.

The Hawkins house was yellow with a brown roof and white trim. In a few places, paint from the trim had dribbled in rivulets onto a picture window. I curbed my wheels, crossed the street to the door, and rang the bell. Inside, a dog began to bark.

Susanna opened the door, looking tired. She was wearing jeans and a blue work shirt with the tail out and the sleeves rolled up, and around her neck was a choker of tiny red and blue beads. Her long brown hair was loose on her shoulders. "Hi, come in. Excuse the confusion," she said, and led me to a tiny living room which was vastly overpopulated by two small dark-haired boys and a large, furry white sheepdog who appeared overjoyed at my presence and wanted to prove it by lunging at me.

"Leave her alone, Curly," Susanna said without notice-able effect. Then, addressing the older of the two children, "Abner, take Curly out back, would you please?" As Abner, whom I guessed to be around four, corralled the dog, I noticed that the smaller boy, about two, had taken the opportunity to begin writing on the wall with a red crayon. From the look of the wall, it wasn't the first time he had tried it. It took Susanna several minutes of persuasion mixed with threats before he was dispatched to play with his brother in the backyard. "Zeke is an individualist, but Abner can handle him for a minute," Susanna said. "Now let's see. Where was the folder I had for you?"

A coffee table in front of the couch was spread with papers, and a cardboard box filled with what appeared to be manuscripts was in the middle of the toy-strewn floor. On an end table I noticed a manila folder. Sitting on top of it was an open jar of peanut butter and a sticky knife. "Is that it?" I asked.

"Oh, yeah." Susanna picked up knife and jar and handed the folder to me. "Hope you don't mind a little peanut butter."

"Not at all." I opened the folder and glanced at its contents. A reprint from *Newsweek* with a photo of Larry posed against the San Francisco skyline, a Xerox from the *Los Angeles Times*. "This will be a big help."

"I hope so." She sat on the arm of a chair. "The only thing is, I hope you don't want to interview me or anything."

I shook my head. "That won't be necessary."

"Good," she said. "See, I know what can happen. People say one thing, but it comes out sounding another way."

"You won't have to worry about that." I felt sorry for her. She looked so fragile, blue viens visible beneath her skin, ash-colored half-circles under her eyes. "What will you do now?"

She picked at a string on her chair. "I don't know. There isn't much money. Everything Larry got, he funneled into the *Times*."

I was taken aback by the frank bitterness in her tone. "The *Times* will continue to publish?"

She shrugged. "I guess it will. I've more or less turned it over to Andrew Baffrey. That paper was Larry's plaything, not mine."

In the downward curve of Susanna's mouth, I read the

bafflement and frustration of someone who has felt unfairly excluded. I could well imagine that Larry Hawkins hadn't been an easy person to live with. Thanking her again, I turned to go, and as I walked to my car I could hear the children shouting, the dog barking in the backyard.

Back home, over a sandwich, I looked at the papers Susanna had gathered for me. There was nothing I didn't already know. As I closed the folder, feeling guilty once again that she had gone to the trouble, the phone rang.

I couldn't remember the last time I'd gotten two phone calls in one day. I answered the kitchen extension. Again, the voice on the other end was unfamiliar, but this time it was male. "Mrs. Longstreet?"

"Yes?"

"Mrs. Longstreet, I have some advice for you. Are you listening?"

The low, expressionless tone made my stomach tighten. "Who is this?"

"Here's the advice," the voice went on. "Stay away from the *People's Times*. If you don't, there could be trouble."

The word "trouble" vibrated in my ear as I heard the receiver go down on the other end of the line. Although I knew the connection was broken I sputtered, "Just who the hell are you?" Nobody answered, so there was nothing left to do but hang up.

SEVEN

After three minutes of blind panic, I started to get angry. Only one person could be responsible for a sinister call telling me to stay away from the *People's Times*, and that person was Richard. Obviously, he was having me followed.

The thought infuriated me as I had rarely been infuriated. Richard had walked out, declared his independence of me and his indifference to my actions, but he wasn't decent enough to leave me my privacy. I went to the living room and looked out the front window. The street was calm, looking almost bleached in the early-afternoon sun. A young woman passed, pushing a stroller. No cars with strangers slouched behind the wheel. No moving curtains in windows across the street.

I went to the glassed-in back room. It was quiet, the only sound an occasional *thwock!* from the tennis courts in the park. Through the luxuriant blossoms of the almond tree I could see the wind-ruffled, greenish waters of Mountain Lake. There were thick clumps of bushes everywhere, tall fir trees, an open-fronted concrete-block structure where old men sat playing checkers. Lots of places to hide. Anybody could hide out there and watch.

The creepy fear that made my hands perspire also fed my rage. I grabbed my purse and slammed out of the house.

My anger was like a balloon, carrying me downtown. I sailed unimpeded through the traffic, constantly checking my rearview mirror to see if there was a suspicious vehicle behind me. It seemed only an instant after I left the house that I was pulling into the outrageously expensive parking lot down the street from Richard's office.

The Redevelopment Agency was located near the Civic Center, in a featureless gray building that could easily have been converted to a cell block. Every atrocity of modern design had been visited on the lobby—glaring fluorescent lights that transformed flesh to dead fish, Muzak, a supergraphic of jagged orange-and-red lightning on the wall. Under the supergraphic, looking even more doddery than when I had last seen him, stood Pop Lewis, the security-guard-cum-doorman.

His hand touched the brim of his uniform cap, and he broke into a welcoming smile that revealed more gums than teeth to fill them. He greeted me with, "Mrs. Longstreet! Why haven't I seen you around lately?"

Wonderful. Pop's refusal to turn up his hearing aid must have prevented his getting in on the office gossip about the divorce. Not waiting for an explanation, he pushed the button to call the elevator for me, then nattered on. "You know, Mrs. Longstreet, my wife never stops talking about those fruitcakes you give us at Christmas. She keeps bothering me about can't I get her your recipe. You know—" The elevator slid open, and I entered gratefully in the full knowledge that Pop wasn't half as impressed with my fruitcakes as he was with the hefty bonus check Richard had always written to go with them.

The seventeenth floor looked exactly as it always had. The carpet was the same bastard combination of yellow and green, the walls still lined with drawings showing the neighborhoods Richard and his henchmen had knocked down or planned to. I walked around the corner to the door marked REDEVELOPMENT AGENCY in gold and, under that, in smaller letters, OFFICE OF THE DIRECTOR.

The receptionist was new and easily cowed, so it was only a few minutes before I was in Richard's suite of offices facing Tabby, his secretary. Tabby was notable for her rhinestone-decorated harlequin glasses, bouffant hairdo, and years-long crush on Richard. She had never liked me. I heard relish in her voice when she said, sweetly, "Mr. Longstreet is in conference at the moment."

Tabby had always intimidated me. Now I realized that it no longer mattered whether she liked me or not. "Well, Tabby," I said, my sweet tone matching hers, "you go tell Mr. Longstreet to get the hell out of conference, because I want to talk to him. It's an emergency."

Her rhinestone-encircled eyes were blank for a moment. Then, with a look at once dignified and murderous, she got up, walked to the closed conference-room door, knocked lightly, and went in.

Soon, she and Richard emerged. The shock of seeing him again nearly undercut my anger, and I felt my mouth go dry. I could tell by the set of his jaw that he was irritated. He glanced at me and said, "Hello, Maggie. Let's go in here for a moment, shall we?"

He was wearing a gray suit and a maroon and gray patterned tie. His hair was a little longer than he used to wear it, and his tan deeper—probably from hours on the tennis court with his athletic young ladylove. Even when tight with displeasure, as it was now, his craggy, elongated face was handsome enough to decorate a carved medieval altarpiece. I had always been willing to forgive him a great deal because of his looks.

As he ushered me into his private office he said, "This had better be important."

"It is." Richard's office was the same, too. The massive desk, the huge schefflera in the redwood tub, the Picasso imitation that hid the wall safe, and the sweep of windows with an incomparable view of the city hadn't changed. The only difference I noted was that my photograph was missing from the bookshelves, although Candace's was still in place.

"Well?" He neither sat nor offered me a chair.

43

"I came to tell you, Richard, that you'd better call off your bloodhounds."

His eyes widened. "What?"

My anger was returning now, giving me energy. "The detective, or whoever it is you've got following me. I want it stopped."

"Maggie, what are you talking about?" Richard's tone was excessively patient, the voice he used with waiters when he sent a dish back.

"I'm talking about the fact that someone is following me. I can't imagine what you have to gain by this kind of harassment. Please call it off."

He spread his arms in an exasperated gesture of having nothing to hide. "I don't know what you're talking about. I've never even considered having you followed."

Of course he would never admit it. I felt my face reddening. "Look. There's no point in denying it. I know I'm being watched."

"You do? *How* do you know?" I saw patronizing pity in his eyes. His tone implied that he was dealing with a lunatic.

"Because . . ." I began furiously, then stopped. If I answered his question, I'd have to tell him about my visit to the *Times.* Presumably, if he'd had somebody make the phone call he already knew of it, but I myself wasn't ready to bring it out into the open yet. "Let's just say I have good reason to think so," I finished weakly.

Now the patronizing air was stronger. "I'm quite sure you do," he said. "But if someone is following you I'm not responsible. You said it yourself. What would I have to gain?"

"I don't know." I made my tone as frigid as I could, but I had lost ground and I knew it.

Richard glanced at his watch. "You know, Maggie, if San Francisco is getting on your nerves, why don't you consider getting away for a while? You could go back to

Mazatlán. You liked Mazatlán, didn't you? Or Greece. We never got to Greece. I could have Tabby make all the arrangements for you."

At this false solicitude, I felt a stirring of something more solid than anger. After a moment I identified it as pure, astringent, honest dislike. "I have no intention of leaving town, Richard," I said. "If my presence is getting on your nerves, *you* go to Mazatlán. And in the meantime, if you're lying and you *have* had someone watching me, I suggest you call him off before I contact the police."

I left him no time to reply and sailed out past the assiduously typing Tabby and down the hall to the elevator.

The afternoon traffic was beginning to fill the streets, and the drive home seemed many times longer than the trip downtown had been. Sitting behind a bus, watching the traffic light ahead change to red once again, I felt my head begin to throb. Maybe it was impossible to get a foothold in the slick surface of Richard's urbanity. He said he wasn't having me watched. Even after being married to him for twenty years, I couldn't tell if he was lying. A stronger throb went through my head, and I put it on his lengthening account. Seeing him again had been a mistake.

When I got home I again looked around for unfamiliar cars or suspicious characters, but the only person in view was the Japanese gardener digging in a neighbor's yard. I climbed wearily to the front door. Who would care if I visited the *Times*? Only Richard. If Richard knew what I was up to, he would care, so Richard must be responsible for the phone call. I should get in touch with the cops. Put the cops on him, let them take care of it. I pictured myself explaining to the police that my husband, a distinguished political figure who played tennis with their bosses, was behind a threatening phone call to me. I pictured the police calling Richard to discuss it with him, and Richard explaining that I was a little bonkers but he'd try to see that they weren't disturbed again.

My head was worse. I kicked off my shoes and lay down on the couch, but I couldn't rest. "There could be trouble," the voice had said. I wouldn't call the police, but there was something I would do. I got up to call Andrew Baffrey.

EIGHT

Andrew sounded surprised, but not displeased, to hear from me. "What can I do for you?"

"It's about what we discussed this morning. Something's happened, and I wanted to ask you—"

"Wait a second," he broke in. "I don't want to dazzle you with cloak-and-dagger tactics, but I'd rather not discuss this on the phone. I was just leaving. Would you like to meet me in a dark alley, or preferably your neighborhood bar, for a face-to-face conversation?"

"There aren't any bars in my neighborhood."

"Too bad for you. I live next door to one. Where do you live, anyway?"

"Presidio Heights. Lake Street. Next to the park."

He laughed. "Anybody tries to put a bar in that neighborhood, the Planning Commission goes into special session to quash the idea. But never mind, here's another suggestion. I have to stop by Susanna Hawkins's, and then I was going to have an early dinner. Why don't you meet me and we'll grab a bite together?"

It would beat a frozen spinach soufflé. "Fine. Where?"

"Have you ever been to the Food as Spiritual Healing Ashram Restaurant?"

"The what?"

"I thought not. You'll love it. It's run by Sufis, or Hare Krishnas, or some sect like that. The best thing about them is they give you lots of food cheap. It's vegetarian. You don't mind vegetarian, do you?"

I didn't mind vegetarian. The restaurant, a tiny hole in the wall near the intersection of Market and Castro streets, had a couple of fresh daisies on every table. Eating my way through a huge plateful of eggplant curry and brown rice that had been served by a shaven-headed Food as Spiritual Healing devotee, I was almost inclined to agree with the printed cardboard placard on the table: A FULL STOMACH; A HAPPY HEART; A SOARING SPIRIT. Certainly the ashram's guru, whose blown-up photograph adorned all four walls, seemed to have eaten himself into a blissful state of benignity and tubbiness. "So what happened?" asked Andrew.

I poured more chamomile tea. "After our conversation this morning, did you talk to Richard? Did you mention what I said to anybody at all?"

He looked properly shocked and offended. "Of course not. I gave you my word, didn't I? Off the record is off the record. Why?"

I told him about the phone call, and my subsequent visit to Richard, finishing, "He claims he isn't having me watched, but if you didn't tell him I came to the *Times* I can't think of any other explanation."

Andrew sat back in his chair, frowning. "I don't like this a bit."

"Neither do I. Threatening phone calls are too much for me."

He swirled the tea in his teacup, staring at it as if he were going to read the stray chamomile blossoms in the bottom. "There's another possible explanation."

"What?"

He set the cup down. "Maybe you aren't the one being watched. Maybe somebody's watching the *Times*."

I considered the idea. "Then the person watching the *Times* would have to know me."

"Know you by sight, anyway. Maybe he's an avid reader of the society pages."

I winced, thinking of myself squinting into the flashbulbs at a ribbon-cutting, the first night of a play, a charity ball. "Even if he did know me, why would he warn me to stay away? It doesn't make sense."

"It sure doesn't." He picked up the cardboard placard and tapped it on the table in a nervous tattoo.

The Indian music playing in the background sounded even more off-key than Indian music usually did. The photographs of the beaming guru had begun to look a little sinister. "I wish . . ." I began, then stopped.

"Wish what?"

"Wish we knew what Larry's story on Richard was all about. That's the only possible connection in all this."

Andrew sat slumped in his chair, still toying with the brochure. A full stomach. A happy heart. A soaring spirit. I hoped I wasn't getting indigestion. At last he reached into the pocket of his jeans, brought out a metal key ring with one key attached, and put it on the table. "Let's go find out," he said.

It was a small, uninteresting-looking key. "What do you mean?"

"This," Andrew said, tapping the key with his finger, "is Larry's key to the cabinet in his office. I just stopped by and picked it up from Susanna. You remember I told you I hadn't gone through Larry's private papers? That's where they are."

"You think he kept the information on Richard there?"

"It's there if it's anywhere. I hadn't checked it out because—well, mainly because I didn't have myself together enough to do it. Susanna had the only key. She's been at the *Times* once since Larry died, but I didn't get it from her then because I wasn't there. She got hysterical and Betsy had to drive her home."

"I remember it well." I told him about Susanna's scene and her subsequent apology.

"Poor Susanna. She hasn't had an easy time." He picked up the key, tossed it once, caught it. "What do you say? Do we go take a look?"

I heard the voice on the telephone. *Stay away from the People's Times. If you don't, there could be trouble.* "Sure. Lead on."

He got up. "I'll drive, and drop you back here afterward."

Folded into his Volkswagen, I shivered. The fog was rolling in, and it would be a damp, chilly night. I felt sad, cut off from everything that had been familiar and comfortable about my life. Other people were at home having a drink, eating dinner, watching the evening news. I was rattling through the dark streets in a Volkswagen with an inadequate heating system, caught in a dim and threatening world of suicide, anonymous phone calls, locked cabinets. The glaring light from a gas station briefly illuminated Andrew's face, and it seemed to me the face of the only friend I'd ever had. My nose was prickling. To keep myself from falling apart, I said, "How do you know Larry kept his private papers in the cabinet, if it was always locked? Maybe he kept drugs in there. Or—pornography, or something."

"The pornography's in a filing cabinet in the newsroom, and Larry had a strict rule about no drugs on the premises," Andrew said. "Larry wasn't much of a doper, and he didn't want any dope hassles. In that cabinet he kept one of those dark red accordian-pleated folders. I've seen him lock it in there lots of times. My impression was that it contained names, phone numbers, rough drafts, working notes, Xeroxes of documents, and stuff like that. He never left anything lying around."

I didn't reply. A dark red folder stuffed with incriminating documents about Richard. *There could be trouble.*

* * *

The *Times* offices were oppressively quiet. Andrew switched on lights as we entered, and I trailed after him to Larry's office. Inside, there was a desk with books and papers stacked on either side of a manual typewriter, shelves along one wall. Behind the desk, two large windows. I walked over to them and looked down. No screens. Below, the alley where Larry had died was lost in blackness.

"Let's see now." Andrew's voice was subdued. The cabinet was built into the bookshelves, and was closed with a padlock. Andrew's hands shook as he tried to fit the key into it. "Dammit," he muttered, wiping his hands on his jeans. He tried again, and this time I heard the tiny click as the key turned. He removed the lock and opened the door. "What have we here," he said, peering inside. He didn't speak for a moment, then stepped back, an indecipherable look on his face. He waved his hand toward the cabinet.

I leaned forward. The cabinet's interior was shadowy, but there was no doubt that it was empty.

NINE

"That's it. It isn't here." Andrew, sitting in Larry's desk chair, closed the bottom drawer of the desk.

"I guess not." I replaced a stack of *Editor and Publisher Yearbook*s. Nothing was on the shelves behind them but a few dust bunnies and a yellowing couple of pages about minority hiring in the Department of Public Works.

In the half hour since we discovered the folder was gone, we had searched the office wordlessly. The door of the cabinet still stood ajar, like a mouth open in accusation. I sat down in the bottom-sprung armchair meant for Larry's visitors. "You're sure nobody has been in here since Larry died?"

"The office hasn't been locked. Anybody could've come in. But nobody would've been able to open the cabinet, that much is for sure."

I cast about for explanations. "Maybe he took the folder home with him. Maybe Susanna has it."

"She would've given it to me. The last thing she cares about is city politics. Besides, it was here the afternoon before he died. He and I had a—a long talk . . ." Andrew's voice quavered. He swallowed and went on. "When I came in, it was on his desk. He picked it up and locked it away. I saw him do it."

"Then somebody was here. Somebody took the folder."

"Looks like it." He got up abruptly and walked toward me, seeming activated by nervous energy. "Say Larry took the folder out again, after I left. He's here late, and he's sitting here with it, and this person comes in, and they have a fight . . ." He leaned and took me by the shoulders, his thumbs pressing in almost painfully. "Do you see?"

Taken aback by his imploring tone, I nodded, and he released me. I did see. The folder was gone. It was probable that someone had stolen it the night Larry died. If, as Andrew obviously believed, the folder contained information on Richard, who was more likely to have stolen it than Richard himself?

I felt a tickle of panic. If Richard had stolen the folder, maybe he had pushed Larry out the window, too. Accusing Richard of murder in the abstract was all very well, but this—this could be more truth than I'd bargained for.

"Maggie, we've got to find out." Andrew's face was fervent, his voice full of conviction. I tried to remember what it was like to be so young, to see everything in the shadowless illumination of certainty. Yet he was right. If Richard had stolen the folder, or done worse things than that, I wanted to know.

Andrew squatted down beside my chair, talking excitedly. "This *proves* that there was something funny about Larry's death. If we can get a line on whoever took that folder we'll confront the person, and—God, what a great story!"

"Stop the presses," I said. "Nothing has been proved. We have a suspicion to follow up, that's all."

"You're right, you're right." He patted my arm, placating the elderly wet blanket. "But how about this," he went on meditatively. "Somebody was here the night Larry died, because the folder's gone and we know Larry didn't jump out the window with it under his arm. Would you agree that if we find the folder we'll be a lot closer to knowing what happened to Larry?"

"Yes."

"And would you agree that Richard is a logical place to start looking?" Andrew's voice was light and steady.

Here was my last chance to change my mind. I didn't. "I agree. Let's tie the folder and Richard together, if we can."

A subtle change came over him, as if somewhere in his body a chronic pain had stopped, allowing him to relax. We looked at each other for a long moment before he said, "Good."

He stood up and started for the door, and I found myself suddenly fretful. "I feel old," I said. "Too old for missing folders, for tracking things down—"

"That's crap," said Andrew cheerfully. "Besides, the word is *mature*. You can never get too mature for anything."

Mature. I wondered if I could even lay claim to that. I got up and followed him to the door. "Something on the order of a ripe Camembert?"

He turned out the light. "Fine wine. The finest fine wine."

When Andrew let me out at my car, near the Food as Spiritual Healing Ashram Restaurant, he said, "You'll get home all right, won't you? Would you like me to follow you and make sure?"

I was demoralized and unnerved, and would have loved for him to follow me. On the other hand, I felt like being alone to think, and Lake Street was probably far out of his way. "No, thanks. I'll be OK." I hoped I was telling the truth.

Driving beneath streetlights surrounded by muzzy, fog-produced haloes, I pondered the question of why I'd married Richard. It wasn't a new subject, having been my constant preoccupation in recent months. The best explanation I had ever come up with was: It seemed like a good idea at the time. He was an extremely attractive man, and his prospects were excellent. If he had been, even then, ruthless and single-minded in the pursuit of his own ends, why—in some circles that was considered a virtue. I had never wondered what shape my own life would take, once we were married. I had known it would simply take the shape of his.

To hell with Richard. What I wanted more than anything was a brandy and hot bath. The thought of these consolations aroused a tentative pleasurable anticipation that was uppermost in my mind when I slammed the garage door and, immediately afterward, felt myself being pulled roughly into the shrubbery beside the garage.

My assailant had a strong grip, and the hand he clamped over my mouth smelled strongly of nicotine. He pulled my head back in a way that made my neck feel very vulnerable and walked me a few feet down the bush-sheltered walkway between my garage and the house next door. I tried vainly to turn my head far enough to look at his face, but succeeded only in smelling his nicotine-loaded breath as he said, "I told you to stay away from the *Times*, didn't I, Mrs. Longstreet?"

He had. The uninflected voice was the same as the one on the phone.

He went on, his moist cigarette breath hot on my neck.

"Did you think I was kidding?" I didn't know why he kept asking questions. I couldn't possibly answer or even nod.

"If you don't pay attention this time, you're really going to be in trouble."

I believed him. The way I saw it, I was in quite a bit of trouble already.

TEN

I was going to kick backward, try to catch his shins. I berated myself for not wearing my tallest, most dangerous heels instead of the sensible stacked ones I had on. I had already swung my foot forward in preparation when the two of us were illuminated by headlights from a car turning into my driveway. The man's hands loosened and I pulled free and turned, glimpsing a narrow face shadowed by a hat. Before he darted toward the back of the garage, the park, the million hiding places there, I got the impression of a sharp nose, and thin lips drawn back in a grimace of surprise.

I scrambled in the opposite direction, toward the front of the house, where the headlights of Andrew's Volkswagen were extinguished just as I rounded the corner babbling incoherently about needing help.

He jumped out of the car. "What's going on?"

"It was a man . . ." I stammered, pointing in the direction he had run.

Andrew took off down the path, and I stood, painfully undecided whether I was more terrified to go with him or stay here by myself. I could hear him thrashing around in the bushes. After a few minutes I also heard a car start somewhere down the street. I was willing to bet it was the narrow-faced man getting away scot-free.

Andrew returned, breathless. "No sign of him. What happened?"

I was vibrating all over. "Not till I've had some brandy."

After the first drink I was down to a slow tremor, and able to tell him the story. Sipping my second, I wandered through the house checking doors and windows and assuring myself that nobody else was skulking ready to spring. "You've got a security system, I assume?" asked Andrew, tagging along.

"The best money can buy." I stopped in front of a door. "Wait. I forgot to check in here." I opened it and peered in.

"The broom closet?"

I studied the vacuum cleaner, the broom, the dustpan, the cans of furniture polish and floor wax. "I'm not taking any chances."

At last I was satisfied that the house was empty. We returned to the living room. "What led you to show up in the nick of time, anyway?" I asked.

"I felt uneasy, letting you off like that. I found a phone booth and looked up your address, thought I'd stop by and check."

"I'm glad you did."

He rolled his glass between his hands. "Have you thought about calling the police?"

"Sure." I'd thought about it a lot. I explained my fear that if I went to the police, Richard would make me look like a paranoid, if harmless, nuisance. I concluded, "So if I tell them, what's accomplished? They probably won't do anything, and we've tipped our hand that we're on to him. For the moment, I'm going to go it alone."

"Not *quite* alone."

"No. I'm glad about that, too."

He breathed deeply, sighed almost, and I thought how his pale skin looked golden, his hair and beard rich brown in the mellow light of the lamp. When he spoke, his voice was soft. "I have to tell you something. I haven't played completely straight with you, Maggie."

The first flutter of disappointment was followed, immediately, by a knifing, heartbreaking sense of betrayal. *I thought you were my friend,* something inside me wanted to scream, while another voice rushed in to say, *Calm down, calm down. You hardly know him.* I managed to ask, "What do you mean?"

He picked at a worn spot on the knee of his jeans, and I noticed again the knobbiness of his wrists. "When you told me you thought maybe Richard Longstreet was mixed up in Larry's death, you were throwing a lifeline to a drowning man. The waters were deep." He hesitated, then went on. "Up to that point I had no doubt, no doubt at all, that Larry's suicide was entirely my fault."

It was the last thing I expected to hear, but in a way I was prepared. Andrew's desperation had been evident when I first met him. Some of his reactions had been odd since. Here was the explanation. "But why?"

He said, tightly, "Because that afternoon, the afternoon before he died, I pushed him to the wall. He was finished and he knew it."

"What are you talking about?"

He finished his drink and placed the glass carefully on the table in front of him, lining it up with the ashtray. "I'm talking about the fact that Larry Hawkins was a blackmailer. The people's protector was no better than any of the crooks he exposed. The crusader was carrying the banner with one hand, while the other was in somebody else's pocket."

"Are you sure?" No doubt I sounded as flat-footed as I felt.

"Of course I'm sure." His voice was charged with bitterness. "I would hardly sit here and tell you something like this if I weren't sure."

I could only blink and mouth questions, having apparently lost the power of rational cognition. "Who was he blackmailing? How do you know?"

He settled back, and I sensed that he was ready to tell the story. "You familiar with the name Joseph Corelli?"

"I don't think so."

"That's not surprising. Corelli doesn't aspire to be a public figure. But I'll bet you know Luigi's Pasta Palazzos, those Italian fast-food places?"

"Sure." It was impossible not to know Luigi's Pasta Palazzos. Their red and white striped awnings graced many San Francisco street corners, always signaling an aroma of garlic and tomato sauce wafting across the sidewalk.

"Corelli is Luigi's. He started the original one, on Columbus Avenue, several years ago, and expanded from there. He made a lot of money. He's the guy Larry was blackmailing."

"What did Larry have on him?"

"I'm still working on that, but I'm positive Larry was taking money from Corelli regularly. It's all down in the books, if you know what you're looking for. It's ironic"— Andrew smiled ruefully—"Larry's the one who taught me how to sift through numbers, how to analyze a balance sheet, how to read documents. My proficiency is what did him in."

Things were moving too fast for me. "How did you find out?"

"I have a friend who works part-time slinging lasagna at the original Luigi's on Columbus. That's where Corelli has his office. Anyway, my friend tipped me off that there were some violations of the health code going on down there. It sounded like a great story, so I started hanging around the various Luigi's branches, striking up conversations with the cooks, seeing if I could see any rat feces, or insect remains, stuff like that—"

"I've eaten my last Luigi's pizza."

"I don't eat there myself, anymore," he agreed. "Anyway, with the help of my friend, I thought I had a dynamite

57

story. I got together an outline and went to Larry, and you know what?"

"What?"

"Larry told me, categorically, to forget the whole thing."

"Did he give a reason?"

"Larry didn't think he owed anybody explanations. He said drop the story, and he expected that to be that. I couldn't accept it, though. I thought maybe he just needed more proof. In my spare time, I kept hanging out down at the Columbus Avenue Luigi's. I figured if I could uncover a really flagrant violation, Larry would have to give in. And guess what happened."

"Larry came in?"

"Right. I happened to see him, and he didn't see me. He was hustling off down the hall to Corelli's office. I watched him go in, and kept an eye on the door until he came out. When he left, I followed him. Right to the bank. What could be more no-class? I would've given Larry credit for a little finesse."

I heard crushing disappointment in Andrew's ironic tone. "Then you started checking the books?"

"Yeah. Once I knew what I was looking for it was easy. He'd been bleeding Corelli for a couple of years. Not for huge amounts, you understand. A few thousand here and there. Maybe ten or twelve thousand in all."

"So you confronted Larry."

"Oh, jeez." Andrew rubbed his eyes. "The thing that sounds stupid and corny is that I looked up to Larry. I really admired the guy and what he was trying to do. That—the way I felt—made it worse. You have to understand I was madder than hell. I had my facts and figures, and I laid it out in front of him. He tried everything. Laughing it off, blustering, insults, telling me I was fired. Through it all, I pushed him to the wall. I didn't know I had it in me to be so ruthless."

He seemed to shrink, even now, from the memory of what he'd done. "It must have been awful," I said.

He nodded slowly. "The worst was when he finally broke. He cried. He said he had to have the money to keep the *Times* going. The *Times* was his life and he had to keep publishing, and hitting up Corelli was the only way to do it, because the *Times* always lost money. It was literally the most painful thing I've ever been through."

I couldn't think of anything to say. Andrew's eyes were red now, staring past me. "I didn't give in," he said hoarsely. "I thought he should have to live by the rules he set up. I told him I was going to call a guy I knew on one of the dailies and give him the story. Larry's enemies would've had a field day. I wasn't sure I'd really do it, but I wanted him to believe me, to spend some time stewing, and then I'd decide. The next morning, he was dead."

Neither of us spoke. Of course this explained why Andrew had been so avidly interested in the fact that somebody else—Richard—might have been involved in Larry's death. Andrew got up and stretched, as if trying to ease the tension in his body. Echoing my thought, he said, "You see that when you came in with your story about Richard I was ripe for it. Anything to get the guilt off my own shoulders."

I was so tired, so overwhelmingly tired that I wasn't sure I could even reply. Debilitating fatigue had seeped into me bone deep as I listened to Andrew's story. "Let's don't talk about it right now. We'll talk tomorrow," I said.

"Right." Andrew sounded as exhausted as I was. I walked to the door with him. Before I let him out he said, "Listen, Maggie . . ."

"Yes?"

"You understand why I confronted Larry the way I did? It seems excusable to you?"

"Under the circumstances, *not* confronting him would have been inexcusable."

He bent and kissed my cheek. I felt for an instant his warm lips, the tickle of his beard. "Thanks," he said. I opened the door, and he stepped out. "Make sure you lock it behind me."

The reminder was unnecessary. As I slid the chain into its little socket, I heard his feet pounding down the steps. The Volkswagen's motor started up, then got fainter as he drove away. After that, everything was quiet.

ELEVEN

Tired as I was, I had suspected I wouldn't sleep, and I didn't. Being grabbed and threatened by a narrow-faced nicotine addict had engendered bodily quivers that wouldn't subside no matter how many deep-breathing exercises I did. I left lights on in every room, and spent approximately half the night checking the windows and doors and the other half wondering if I should check them again.

During the time I was lying wide-eyed in bed I had plenty to think about. Larry Hawkins was a blackmailer. As he raged at others for doing favors in return for influence or money, he was playing the game himself. Obviously, Larry had seen his mission as higher than the rules governing petty, fallible mortals. Reading the *Times*, I had recognized his vision of himself as scourge to the powerful, champion of the powerless. In the face of that vision, if it took a little graft to get the job done—well, the job was the important thing.

Then there was Richard. There were dozens, hundreds, of possible explanations for the disappearance of Larry's folder, but I didn't have to worry about those. I had to consider only the single possibility, no matter how small, that Richard had taken it. I asked myself, in the glare of the kitchen at three A.M. as I checked the back door for the fourth time, how I would ever find out if he had.

Wandering through the house, I thought about my attacker, saw again his sharp-nosed, thin-lipped face. I wanted to scream "How dare you!" like an uppity lady in an outmoded comedy. How dare he touch me, how dare he threaten me? What a strange and unexpected turn my life had taken. None of this would have happened if I'd still been married to Richard. "Don't attend the Museum Guild again or you'll be in trouble, Mrs. Longstreet"? Hardly likely.

At five A.M. I decided this was ridiculous. I doubted my anonymous enemy would show up now, and at this rate lack of sleep would kill me before he got the chance. Leaving all the lights on, I took a pill and barricaded myself in the bedroom, pulling my antique rosewood desk in front of the door. I put my head under the pillow, and in fifteen or twenty minutes I was asleep.

Later I awoke, startled, convinced I had heard something. The quality of the light in the room told me it was late morning. Surely there hadn't been a sound. I tried to relax, and for a moment almost succeeded. Then I heard the footsteps. Someone was walking through the house, coming closer and closer. The steps came to my door and stopped. I sat up in bed, rigid with horror, convinced that in a moment he would shoot through the door, or batter it with his shoulder the way they did on television. Expecting cataclysm, I heard the politest of taps and a voice calling, "Mother?"

Candace. She must have driven up from Stanford. For a confused instant, I thought the man had to be there too, perhaps holding my daughter hostage. But when the imperious "Mother, are you in there?" came, I knew she wasn't in danger. She had simply unlocked the back door with her key and come in.

"Just a second," I called. It was a considerable effort for

my fright-weakened muscles to move the desk, but I finally managed it and opened the door to greet Candace, who was wearing the frown she assumed when I had done something to embarrass her.

"Why are all the lights on?" she asked, walking into the bedroom. Taking in the displaced desk, she said, "You had that in front of your door? Good grief, Mother, what's going on? Are you hallucinating or something?"

Candace was named for Richard's mother, and she had inherited that estimable woman's penchant for speaking her mind and damn the consequences. In appearance, fortunately, she was like Richard rather than the old lady. Perhaps this physical resemblance had contributed to the closeness that had always existed between them. "Hello, Candace," I said, kissing her cheek. "You're looking wonderful."

She was. Her shoulder-length blonde hair was beautifully groomed, her makeup understated and impeccable, and no particle of lint clung to her plum-colored blazer and gray slacks. But she wasn't in the mood for idle maternal admiration. "Daddy called me yesterday," she said briskly. "I tried to get you last night, but you didn't answer."

"I got in rather late."

"Mother, he said you came crashing into his office yesterday while he was in a meeting, insulted Tabby, insisted on talking to him, and then accused him of having you followed. I couldn't believe it."

"You might as well. It's a fairly accurate representation of what happened."

"Oh, *Mother.*"

If tones could wither, I would've been a shriveled leaf on the bedroom carpet. "Candace, I just got up. Before we go on with this, I insist on having a cup of coffee. Or, listen. We'll go to La Belle Bretagne and have crepes for brunch. How about that?"

It was a play for time. The words *brunch* and *crepes* were an assured sop to Candace's notions of sophistication. The frown on her face smoothed out a little. If I were capable of such a suggestion I must have a shred of sanity left. "OK," she agreed. Relieved, I went to pick out something to wear.

The atmosphere at La Belle Bretagne was as chichi as usual—bright green walls, tiny glass-topped white wicker tables, bentwood chairs, and lots of stylish ladies drinking Bloody Marys. Candace and I followed the maitre d' to a white latticed booth that resembled an Easter basket. Although feeling less than stylish myself, I decided I still rated a Bloody Mary, and ordered one, while Candace settled for a glass of white wine. "So, how are classes going?" I asked, with my best imitation of brightness.

Candace wasn't to be deterred. "I cut today because Daddy asked me to talk to you. I think he's worried."

Leave it to Richard to call out his most potent ally at the first sign of trouble. "Worried?"

"This business about somebody following you. It's so paranoid. Daddy doesn't know what to think, because he certainly hasn't had you followed. And this morning. My goodness, Mother, you were *barricaded* in your room. Do you really believe someone is after you?"

Candace's expression revealed that she herself didn't believe it for a minute. I was tempted to tell her about the phone call and my lurking attacker, just to see if I could wipe the pitying look off her pretty face. If I told her, though, I'd also have to tell her that I suspected Richard of some unsavory activities, and I wasn't ready to do that. I tried for a measured tone in my response. "I've had good reason to think someone is keeping an eye on me. If your father says he isn't responsible, perhaps he's telling the truth. In any case, I have no plans for a repeat performance of yesterday. You might reassure him on that score."

She leaned toward me. "Daddy suggested you get away for a while. Don't you think that's a thoughtful idea? You could go somewhere and rest, see the sights. It would give you a new perspective."

"Since he told you everything else, he must have told you I rejected that plan yesterday. If I need a new

63

perspective, I'll have to find it right here. And no, I don't think it's particularly thoughtful that he wants me out of his hair."

Our spinach-and-mushroom crepes arrived, and while the waitress put them down Candace was primly silent. As soon as we were alone again she said, with evangelical sincerity, "I wish you'd try not to be so negative, Mother. Daddy didn't intend to hurt you. He just needed his own space, don't you see? Couldn't you at least make an effort to understand?"

His own space my eye. "Believe me, Candace, that's exactly what I'm trying to do."

Later, standing under the drifting pale mauve flowers of the Japanese magnolia while I watched her green MG turn the corner, I wondered if all parents were as baffled by their children as I was by Candace. She had been a child during San Francisco's hectic ferment of the sixties, and at the time I had been profoundly grateful that she was too young to participate in the Summer of Love, live in a crash pad in the Haight, join the Free Speech Movement at Berkeley, or riot at San Francisco State. Yet it seemed to me odd that such cataclysms had washed past her, leaving not a single discernible trace. Unless her present character *was* the trace they had left.

Candace could be fun. On good days we could shop together, laugh, go to a movie, make a quiche, even talk a little. On the whole, though, I had always represented bedtime-and-take-your-medicine to Candace, while Richard was walks in the park and a new puppy. Now, he was Sensitive Daddy, needing his own space—with a woman in it very little older than Candace herself—and I was Poor Paranoid Mother.

The MG was gone now, and its going had left a pain that made me press my hand against my chest.

TWELVE

Before depression could invade me completely, Andrew called. "We've got a mess down here you wouldn't believe," he said with obvious relish. "Somebody broke in last night. When Betsy got here this morning, filing cabinets and desk drawers were open, papers scattered around, garbage cans emptied out. But get this—nothing missing as far as we can tell."

"You think they were after the folder?"

"Could've been. At least you and I left the cabinet open last night, so they didn't have to take an axe to it."

"Did you call the police?"

"Nope."

"Why not?"

"Two reasons." I could picture him ticking them off on his fingers. "First, the police are not fond of the *People's Times*. You remember our series about cops drinking on the job? And the Gilhooly investigation that Larry took apart move by move, showing how inept they had been? This would be an opportunity for them to poke around here and look for a chance to get even, and who needs that? Also, if we can get this together ourselves it'll be a fantastic story, and calling the cops is tantamount to giving it away to the dailies."

"I see." I did see, but it felt strange. I had always been a law-abiding citizen and now, at my age, I seemed to have developed a mistrust of the police as fervent as that of any member of the counterculture. Still, what to do about his break-in was Andrew's decision, not mine.

"I have something else to tell you," he went on. "I did some mild snooping around Richard's office this morning. Nothing too impressive, just posed as an Olivetti repairman looking for a nonexistent city agency. I ended up taking the receptionist out for coffee."

I suppressed a twinge of resentment that Andrew hadn't consulted with me before taking action. "Fast worker."

"All in the line of duty. Let's see . . ." I heard a muffled fumbling on the other end of the line. "I have a list here of the people Richard sees and speaks with on the phone most frequently. There's a Tompkins, a guy named Standish—"

"Jack Standish is his lawyer. I think Tompkins is a tax man."

"Good. What about a lady named Diane something?"

Could I sound casual? "That's the girl he's living with."

After a short silence, Andrew said, "Oh." He cleared his throat and went on, "Next on the list is Jane Malone. I know who she is. Executive vice president, Basic Development. And then we have—"

"Jane Malone?" The name was familiar. "Wasn't she the woman who offered her cabin to the Channel Eight guy, Kenneth MacDonald, and Larry wrote a story about it?"

"Hey, that's right. Ken hasn't worked since. Spends all his time boozing out on Union Street, when he's not down here demanding a retraction."

"Do you think he'd know anything? Since he and Richard are both involved with this Jane Malone?"

"I think a better question is whether Ken has *ever* known anything, including the time of day. You're right, though. Maybe I'd better talk to him. OK, now—"

"Why don't *I* talk to him?" My jaw was tensing up. I had started this investigation, after all. I wasn't in the mood to let Andrew steamroll me with his flashy journalism technique and his twenty-five-year-old enthusiasm.

"Dynamite." Competition, apparently, was not uppermost in Andrew's mind. "He hangs out at the Golden Raintree, on Union Street. In fact, after you see him why don't you come by here, and we'll compare notes. But first, see if these other names mean anything to you."

None of them did, and in half an hour I was engrossed in the search for a parking place near Union Street—a quest that could easily last hours, or even years. Crawling for the fifth or sixth time down boutique-lined blocks where handmade leather clothing, overpriced kitchenware, and heavily refurbished antiques were displayed with the maximum possible chic, I began to wonder if Andrew hadn't tricked me into insisting I must have this assignment. I finally found a semilegal space on a side street only seven blocks away and joined the honeymooners from Chicago and Kiwanians from Des Moines on the sidewalk.

In common with Union Street itself, the Golden Raintree aspired to class but was a little too flashy to achieve it. It was the perfect backdrop, in fact, for Ken MacDonald. A stylized, many branched tree was painted in gold on the front window. The interior decoration consisted of mirrors, stained glass, dark wood, and enough ferns to outfit twenty forest glades.

Although the place was crowded, I spotted Ken immediately. He was sitting at a table near the window, staring at the drink in front of him. His profile seemed to have disintegrated even more in the short time since I last saw him, and his head was tilted toward his chest, creating a double chin. I walked over and said, "You're Ken MacDonald, aren't you?"

He didn't get up, in fact barely looked up, but unsteadily held out his hand. "Channel Eight."

"My name is Maggie. We met at the *People's Times* the other day."

"That crummy rag." He continued to contemplate his drink.

I could see that no engraved invitations would be issued.

I pulled out a chair and sat down. "I understand Larry Hawkins wrote a story about you."

For reply, Ken got out a cigarette and lit it, exhaling smoke in a long sigh. "It was my image," he said.

"What?"

"My image. You know. Clean, rock-solid, upright, intellectual. All that." He drank. "That's how Larry did me in."

Ken apparently lived to recount his problems with Larry. Fine. When he got to the appropriate point in the story, I'd drop in a question about Richard. I didn't intend to listen without a drink, though. Signaling a waiter, I ordered a Bloody Mary. By the time it arrived, Ken was getting querulous. "Other guys can get away with all kinds of things," he complained. "Not me. I had to get stuck with an upright image."

"The story about you wasn't a lie, then?"

Ken was warming to the subject. "I'll tell you something, lady. There are lies and there are lies. Yeah, I spent two weeks at Tahoe in that cabin. I don't deny it."

"But then—"

He held up his hand. "Let me finish. That place was offered to me by a guy named Nick Fulton. Hell, I guess he may have mentioned it, but I didn't realize he worked for Basic Development. He used to hang out in here, matter of fact." Ken glanced around as if he dared Nick Fulton to come in and belly-up to the bar. "So I went up there. I mean, the place wasn't any palace, you can take my word for it. The thing that's so insulting"—he pointed his finger at me—"is that everybody believes I'd sell out for something so damn *small*."

"Well, you did come out in favor of the Golden State Center right after you got back. You have to admit it looks bad."

"You don't have to believe me, but I swear to God this is true." He looked as pious as a man is able to look when he can hardly sit upright. "That was sheer coincidence. I really

68

do think they ought to build that goddamn development. Christ"—he grasped my arm, his face pink with earnestness—"It means jobs, it means a new look for the waterfront, it'll give the city a tremendous boost all the way around."

"And you never discussed it with Nick Fulton?"

He let go of my arm, looking hurt. "I'm not saying we never discussed it. Could be we did. But Nick never emphasized that he worked for Jane Malone. At least, if he did I don't remember it."

"Do you remember if Nick ever mentioned Richard Longstreet?"

Having delivered his defense, Ken had apparently lost interest in the conversation. He lapsed back into his brooding pose and when he answered it was without interest. "The Redevelopment honcho? Sure. Nick told me it was his private understanding that Longstreet was extremely high on the project. It must have been true, too. The proposals went through his office and the Board of Supervisors like greased lightning." He finished his drink and signaled the bartender. "And that," he said with finality, "is one in the eye for the Sierra Clubbers."

"I guess it is."

"If that little fucker Larry Hawkins hadn't started snooping around, everything would've been fine."

"He's dead now."

"It's a damn good thing for San Francisco that he is. I'm only sorry somebody didn't string him up by the balls."

Ken was drifting away from me, back into his boozy private realm of hatred. I reached for my purse, but he stopped me, saying, "It's on me."

I got up. "Thanks."

His eyes were bloodshot in his doughy face. "You remember what I told you, now."

"About stringing Larry up by the balls?"

"No, no, no." He shook his head a number of times.

"About the image. The upright, intellectual image I had. That's what did me in. Remember?"

"I won't forget."

Outside, Union Street was hazy in the waning sun. I looked back at Ken through the window. He was staring at his drink, his lips pursed, shaking his head. I turned and hurried toward my car.

THIRTEEN

By the time I reached the *Times* office the sun was gone and a chilly spring twilight was descending. The evening fog had started to roll in, and the blackened edifices that lined Cleveland Street looked sinister and cold. My head bent against the buffeting wind, I hurried into the *Times* building, intent on talking with Andrew. In my rush, I nearly tripped over two bare feet.

The feet belonged to a figure huddled like a sack in the doorway. This was too much for my already overburdened nerves, and I let out a shriek of fright that reverberated like a cymbal crash in the little foyer.

"Jesus, lady, cool out a little," a soft voice said. The figure stirred and coalesced in the dim light. It was a girl, chubby and barefooted, wearing a dirt-streaked T-shirt and Indian-style white cotton pants with a drawstring at the waist. She sat on the floor, her tousled dark hair blending with the wall's dingy gray, her eyes dark blotches in her grimy face.

She was about Candace's age. "Aren't you cold?" was the first thing I thought of to say.

"No, not cold. Not a bit cold." Her voice had an indistinct, singsong quality. I thought she was probably on some sort of drug.

Thank God it wasn't Candace. "You shouldn't sit here. It's cold, and it's getting dark."

The girl rested her head on her knees. Her voice was a mumble I had to kneel to hear. "Cold and dark. You should ask Larry about cold and dark. That's what it's like where he is." She rocked back and forth and then began to cry, her shoulders shaking.

Her plump, little-girl hands were over her face. Tattooed on the back of the left one was a small red apple with two green leaves. "Do you work for the *Times*?"

She continued to cry. Kneeling there in the semidarkness, I wondered what I could do to comfort her. If this girl were Candace, I would want someone to try to help. While I dithered, her sobs subsided and she looked at me. "You'll get your fancy clothes dirty, here on the floor," she said.

I was aware of my beige suit, the silk scarf at my neck, my warm shoes. "Can't I take you home? Do you have friends upstairs at the *Times*?"

"The only person I ever cared about is dead," she said dully.

The young are so dramatic. "You're talking about Larry Hawkins?"

"Larry." The soft reverence in her tone would have been more fitting in church.

Her bare feet were making me shiver. It was time to be authoritarian. "You can't stay here. I'm going to drive you home. Where do you live?"

It worked. She got to her feet and stood swaying in the doorway. "Not far."

The girl drifted along listlessly beside me, her eyes half closed. She had a soft, teddy-bear look, and I hoped that someone, somewhere, was wondering where she was. When she got into the car she surprised me by saying, "What's your name?"

"Maggie Longstreet. What's yours?"

"September. September Apple. Look. Here's my trademark." She held up her hand for my inspection.

I looked at the apple tattoo. "Very pretty." September Apple? Surely Betsy had mentioned September Apple, saying September and Larry had a terrible fight the day Larry died. I started the car. "Are you a writer?"

She was looking out the window. "I wrote something once. It was for Larry. Just for Larry. But he hated it. He hated it and he died. Just like that."

"You mean you wrote a story for the *Times*?"

"Yeah." She sighed. "It was about the poetry scene in San Francisco. There's a ton of poets here, you know?"

"I'm not sure I realized—"

"A ton. Some of them write one way, and some write another way. Some of them hate each other, and some love each other. They have readings, and put out magazines, and publish little booklets of their stuff, and nobody else in the whole world knows it's even going on. It's—a scene. A poetry scene."

"Sounds like an interesting article."

"Larry couldn't have cared less about poetry himself, but Andrew Baffrey convinced him it was a good idea." September was becoming more animated and coherent. "Man, I worked on that sucker for *months*. I trekked all the way to Marin for a reading once. I really busted my ass. Turn right at the next corner."

I turned. "So how did it come out?"

She hesitated. "That's the thing." She gave her body a little restless toss. "While I worked on the story, I got an idea."

"What was that?"

"I thought, if this article is going to be *about* poetry, maybe it should be written *in* poetry." She looked at me sideways, obviously expecting a comment.

"Original concept." The reason for her altercation with Larry was becoming clearer all the time.

"Go left up here, and it's the second house. Yeah, I

thought it was original too, so I wrote it that way. And he hated it." She began to sniffle.

I searched for some inane reassurance. "You can't take these things to heart." Quelling my private doubts, I went on, "Other editors might feel differently."

We were in the Haight, near the Golden Gate Park Panhandle. I pulled up in front of the house, a rambling, tumbledown Victorian which had evidently been divided into flats. September made no move to get out of the car. Tears were rolling down her cheeks now. Her innocent-looking face reminded me of a child's. "It wasn't the story so much," she gasped. "It was that Larry said he didn't want to fuck me anymore."

An innocent child. All I could manage in response to this revelation was to search my purse for a Kleenex, hand it to her, and say, "He didn't?"

She blew her nose copiously. "I knew it wouldn't last. I had heard it never did with him. But I still couldn't stop myself from—from—"

"This type of—um—affair was a regular thing with Larry?" I interjected before she could break down again.

"Oh sure," she said, wiping her nose. "Having a lot of women was a big macho thing for him. He was such a creep, such an awful creep. How could I have gotten mixed up with such a creep?"

That, I reflected, was a question women had been asking themselves down through the centuries. Women including me. "What about Larry's wife?" I asked.

September looked confused, as if I'd suddenly changed the subject to the latest Watergate revelation or the new season at the opera. "What about her?"

"Did she know what he was doing?"

"Could be. Most everybody did." Her indifference was obvious.

"What about Andrew Baffrey? Did he know?"

"Andrew? Probably. Although who knows? When Larry and I were together, Larry used to laugh at Andrew and call him Brother Andrew the Puritan, because Andrew was such a straight arrow. I guess now Andrew's having the last laugh, huh?"

I was upset and irritated at the thought of Andrew being ridiculed. "I don't think he's laughing," I said stiffly.

"I didn't mean laughing, exactly," September said. "But look where Larry is and look where Andrew is. Do you see what I mean?"

Look where Larry is and look where Andrew is. She opened the door, thanking me for the ride. I watched her climb the steps and go into the house. Her feet looked bluish white.

Back at the *Times*, I found a comfortable buzz of late-afternoon activity. Betsy's desk was messier than before because a coffee can filled with wilting red and pink carnations was sitting on top of the regular clutter. "Aren't they great?" she said. "There's a guy who comes by selling old flowers. We bought them all."

Most desks in the newsroom were adorned with carnations, and the flowers added their delicate scent to the normal one of dust and humanity. Since the place looked no more disorderly than usual, I surmised that the aftereffects of the break-in were minimal.

Two pink carnations drooped over Andrew's desk. When I walked in he was staring abstractedly at them, his fingers poised on his typewriter keys. He glanced up and said, "One second," then burst into a rattle of typing. After a minute or two he stopped, stared at the carnations again, and said, "Oh, hell. It'll have to do." Pulling the sheet from his typewriter he dropped it into a wire basket and said, "Sometimes you have to go with what you've got."

"The *Times* is taking the breaking-and-entering in stride."

"Betsy and I had the place pretty straight by the time anybody else got here, and we didn't make an issue of it. The last thing the *Times* needs right now is a wave of hysteria. What's with you?"

"I just had an interesting conversation downstairs." I told him about meeting September Apple, but didn't mention Brother Andrew the Puritan. When I finished, he nodded.

"I knew Larry screwed around a lot. I always figured it was his business, as long as it didn't hurt the *Times*."

"For somebody so intolerant of weakness in other people, Larry had plenty of vices of his own."

"For Larry, it was different. It was different because Larry was Larry, and everybody else was everybody else." He put his feet on the desk. "Learn anything from Ken MacDonald?"

"He said Nick Fulton, who works for Jane Malone at Basic Development, told him Richard was high on the Golden State Center. He also pointed out how fast the plans got approval from Redevelopment and the Board of Supervisors."

Andrew scratched his beard. "Maggie, I'll bet there's something there. I feel it in my gut. The Golden State Center is the biggest project Basic's ever gotten into. If they had Richard in there leaning on people for them—"

"Using his influence to get the Golden State Center through? In return for what?"

Andrew shrugged. "I don't know. I wish that damn folder hadn't disappeared."

Since the night before, a thought had nibbled at the edge of my consciousness. While I had talked with Candace, and Ken, and September, it was there. I had been reluctant to look at it, but now I decided to bring it out. "We could try getting the folder back."

"Great," said Andrew in mock congratulations. "I wish you'd thought of that sooner."

"Scoff away, but I know Richard. If he took that folder I think I know what he'd do with it."

He was suddenly attentive. "What?"

"He'd put it in the wall safe at his office. He was always proud of having a safe. Considered it a status symbol."

"Some status symbol. But safecracking isn't one of my specialties. Do you have any talent in that line?"

"I've got better. I've got the combination."

Andrew's look was extremely gratifying. As I watched his jaw drop, I remembered when Richard had given the combination to me. Five years ago, right after he became redevelopment director and moved into his new office, he had taken on, for a few weeks, a ponderous gravity which he must have considered commensurate with his new title. One day, with quiet pomp, he had presented me with a sheet of paper I was to keep "just in case." On it he had written all his credit card numbers, our bank-account and safe-deposit-box numbers, a list of insurance policies, and other similar information. At the bottom of the page was the safe combination. Most of it was out of date now, but surely safe combinations didn't get changed every day of the week. And the paper, I knew, was in the top drawer of my desk underneath stacks of canceled checks, where it had lain undisturbed since Richard gave it to me.

"You're absolutely incredible," Andrew said.

Basking in his admiration, I grew expansive. "This is my plan," I said, not knowing until that moment that I actually had one. "Richard usually leaves his office at four-thirty and meets some business associate or other at the Yacht Club for a drink. Tabby, Richard's secretary, leaves at five. Pop Lewis, the doorman, is on duty till six. He doesn't know about the divorce, and I can probably convince him to let me borrow a key to Richard's office. What do you think?"

Andrew still looked stunned, but I could see excitement spreading over his face. "What do I think? I think it's a goddamn stroke of *genius*." He glanced at his watch. "It's five now. Great. I'll follow you home while you get the combination, and then I'll drive you to the agency. I'm the wheel man, you might say."

I looked at him blankly. "You mean now?"

"Sure. Why not?" He stood up. "We'd better get moving."

It was one thing to speculate boastfully about searching Richard's office and quite another to find myself being hustled out the door to do it. My knees were unsteady, I noted almost academically as we waited for the elevator. "What if I find the folder?" I asked. "What then?"

"Take it. What's he going to do, call the cops?"

Take it. Fabulous. Driving home, with Andrew's Volkswagen trailing me, I considered trying to lose him and go somewhere for a quiet dinner. When some women get divorced they go back to school, I thought. Some do volunteer work at the hospital, or join communes and learn to birth calves. Some have affairs with inappropriate men. My new interest is burglary. Maggie Longstreet, former wife and mother, past president of the Museum Guild, now starting a career as a second-story woman.

Rain had started to spit against the windshield. The wind was high. It was perfect weather for embarking on a life of crime.

FOURTEEN

By the time I reached home, I realized it was crazy. I wasn't about to go out and burgle Richard's office. Certainly not. So why was I going to the bedroom and getting the safe combination from the rosewood desk? Why was I searching in the top of the closet for my large flowered straw shopping bag from Mexico, a monstrosity Candace had given me when she was ten? And, most pertinent of all, why was I coolly slipping on a pair of black kid gloves?

I checked myself in the mirror. A society matron out on a

shopping spree, looking a bit grim around the eyes and mouth, as if she had discovered the perfect outfit and the store didn't have her size. The only jarring note was the shopping bag. Not only was it ugly, it was also empty.

Searching around, I found a couple of I. Magnin's paper bags the cleaning woman had saved for some reason, stuffed them with wadded-up newspaper, and dropped them into the Mexican carryall. Much more realistic. After retying the scarf around my neck to make it look more criminally jaunty, I locked the house and joined Andrew, who had been waiting in the car.

"Gloves. Wow," he said.

"Don't 'gloves wow' me. I'm scared enough as it is."

We rolled out of the driveway. "I have one piece of advice for you if you're picked up for this," he said.

"Tell me."

"Stonewall it."

"Very funny, G. Gordon. Or was that Ehrlichman?" I really wasn't up to jokes. Freezing cold one minute and sweaty the next, I sat semicatatonic with fear as Andrew maneuvered us through the rush-hour traffic. It was still raining fitfully. I wondered what would happen if Richard were still there, working late for a change; if somebody came in while I was opening the safe; if the folder wasn't in the safe, and I'd come this far for nothing. Andrew pulled the car into a loading zone half a block from Richard's office. I stared at him in stark terror.

"Hey, Maggie," he said, touching my cheek. "You don't have to go if you don't want to."

The palm of his hand felt so comforting that I wanted to collapse against it. Afraid I might do just that if I waited any longer, I opened the door and, dragging the shopping bag, plunged into the drizzle.

Pop Lewis was sitting in a folding chair next to the sign-in desk looking half asleep, but when he saw me he went into his usual thanks-for-the-fruitcake routine.

My own manner was as cloyingly sweet as I could make

78

it, considering I had to shout to overcome his deafness. "Pop, I'm afraid I've done something awfully stupid," I shrieked. "Richard and I were supposed to meet some people for drinks. I waited half an hour, and I *must* have gone to the wrong place, and I don't know where they are. If I could go up and glance at Richard's calendar—"

I put on a look of desperate pleading. Pop smiled and nodded. "You go right ahead, Mrs. Longstreet."

We stood for a moment—Pop smiling, me desperate. "But I don't have a key to Richard's office," I bawled. "May I borrow yours?"

Pop's ginger eyebrows came together. "I can't do that, Mrs. Longstreet. The building managers are very clear that those keys are never to leave my person."

Silly, hidebound man. I wanted to shake him. Before I could ponder my next move he said, "I could take you up and let you in, though."

What an old dear he was. Overcoming an impulse to smother him in embraces, I said, "*Could* you? That would be wonderful!"

When Pop opened the door, the office was dark. No late workers, thank God. He snapped on the light and showed every intention of following me in, but I blocked his progress by standing in front of him, putting my hand on his shoulder, and exerting a gentle pressure toward the door while I said, "Thanks, Pop. The door will lock again when I close it, won't it? I don't want to keep you from your post and get the building managers upset."

This sent him nodding and waving toward the elevator. With a feeling of suffocation, I walked quickly down the hall to Richard's office and opened the door.

It was empty. I switched on the desk lamp, put down my shopping bag, and got the combination out of my purse. The only sound was the faint rattling of the paper as it shook in my hand. The Picasso imitation swung out easily from the wall to reveal the safe.

Rushing furiously, I twirled the dial, went through the

combination, and pressed the handle. It didn't move. I closed my eyes and felt sweat breaking out all over my body. After forcing myself to breathe deeply, I tried again. I spun the dial and went through the combination, whispering the numbers under my breath. I pressed the handle. The safe opened.

Inside were white stacks of documents. For the first time it occurred to me that Richard might have taken Larry's papers out of the damn folder. I didn't have time to go through all this stuff to look for them. I picked up a stack of what looked like reports, but couldn't focus on the printing on the cover.

Then I saw it. Back in the back, almost hidden, was an accordion-pleated folder. At the sight, I was instantly calm. I no longer cared if anyone came in. I took the folder, replaced the stack of reports, closed the door, turned the dial. In a second, the painting was back in place. I put the folder in the shopping bag and arranged the I. Magnin bags on top.

Then, because it didn't matter anymore, I stood leafing through Richard's leather-bound desk calendar. Whom had he been seeing since we broke up, I wondered idly. The appointments were written in his precise hand, keeping well within the little white squares: "Decorator with Diane," "J. Malone re Golden St. Cntr," three February days with a line drawn through them and "Dallas" written on the line. And what was this? A terse "Corelli" in January. Joseph Corelli? I flipped through the pages. Yes, here it was again, this time "J. Corelli." In fact, according to his calendar, Richard had seen Corelli three or four times in the past two months. Wondering what business Richard would have with Larry's blackmail victim, I turned off the desk light and left the office. I turned off the light in the outer office, too, and shut the door behind me. I was in the hall, and the hall was empty. I had gotten away with it.

FIFTEEN

"Careful. There's a bulb burned out. The stairs are dark," Andrew said.

Not only were the stairs dark; they smelled strongly, but not unappetizingly, of salami, thanks to the Italian delicatessen on the ground floor. Clutching my shopping bag like a housewife bringing home the evening's pot roast, I followed Andrew up and waited while he dug in his pocket for his key.

Andrew lived in North Beach not far from the intersection of Columbus and Broadway, where Carol Doda's neon nipples blinked through the now-driving rain and barkers with their coat collars turned up lounged in the doorways of dives advertising NUDE COLLEGE COEDS and ORIENTAL SEX ACTS. The decision to open the folder at his apartment had been made on the basis of his place being closer than mine. He was obviously in a fever of curiosity. "Be it ever so humble," he said, opening the door.

Humble was a fairly good word for it. The place didn't look dirty, or especially threadbare, so much as simply drab. The lumpy-looking brown couch, the scarred coffee table holding a small portable television set, the paper-littered card table with a typewriter on it, all bespoke someone who didn't spend too much time thinking about his surroundings. There were two colorful objects in the room: a pale blue stained-glass butterfly hanging in a window, and a huge ginger-colored cat not so much perched on as spilling over the sill below it. When we walked in the cat gave us a bottomless green stare.

"Maggie, meet A. J.," Andrew said.

"A. J.?"

"His full name is A. J. Liebling, but you can call him A. J..We're pretty chummy and informal here, aren't we, old buddy?"

A. J. made no reply. "Nice cat," I said.

"Most of the time. He did throw up in my typewriter once. That was hard to forgive."

Andrew took the Mexican carryall, and I watched him toss the I. Magnin bags on the floor and pull out the folder. I still had the disconnected feeling that had come over me when I'd found the folder in Richard's safe. I realized that I wasn't nearly as anxious as Andrew to see what was inside. I walked to the window and touched the butterfly. "How pretty."

He glanced up. "My former girlfriend gave it to me just before she took off to seek big bucks in Iran. She's an engineer."

I scratched A. J.'s head and felt him start to purr. Andrew was fumbling with the folder's knotted strings as eagerly as if they had been ribbons on a long-expected present. "Come on," he said, patting the couch. "Now we'll see."

I crossed and sat down while he pulled papers from the folder and put them down between us. The papers weren't in any obvious order. Some were covered with the positive handwriting I remembered from Larry's suicide note. There were lists of names and phone numbers and what looked like hieroglyphics, photocopied documents, and a four- or five-page typescript which Larry had amended heavily with a black felt-tipped pen. One thing was certain. They were about Richard. The name "Richard Longstreet" jumped at me from almost every page. Some of the photocopies were of letters on his letterhead. Picking one up, I read it. It was addressed to Richard's tax man. Richard was planning to become a partner in an industrial park currently being built in Dallas, and wanted the accountant to tell him what the tax ramifications would be. Innocuous enough, surely.

I put the letter down and picked up a page of handwritten notes headed "Partners in Framton Associates." Underneath was a list of names, some with notations beside them like "cattle" and "dept. store—same name." Circled on the list was "Redfern, Inc." Next to this entry Larry had written, "J. Malone." Jane Malone, of course. The Basic Development executive. But what was Framton Associates? I found the answer in another letter, from a Bill Framton to Richard, welcoming Richard into partnership in their new project in Dallas.

Now it was getting clear. Richard had invested in a Dallas industrial park, becoming partners with Jane Malone, while here in San Francisco as redevelopment director, he was supposed to regulate and oversee Malone's Golden State Center project. Conflict of interest. How could Richard have been so stupid?

Andrew, meanwhile, had been reading the typescript. "Wow," he said reverentially. "Larry did a real job on this. A hell of a job."

"How did he get this information?"

"Some of it's a matter of public record. The rest—the letters and stuff—I don't know. Maybe somebody who works for Richard doesn't like him, and was willing to help Larry out."

Richard had a new receptionist, I remembered. The former one might have succumbed to Larry's blandishments or charms.

"Well, it was idiotic of Richard," I said. "He should've been more careful about his investments."

Andrew's face took on a wary look. "Maggie, you don't think Richard invested in that Dallas venture by mistake, do you?"

"Well—I guess not. Of course it's conflict of interest. Clearly."

Andrew put the papers down. "Let me ask you this.

What does Richard make a year? Sixty thousand? Seventy?"

"Something like that."

"According to Larry"—Andrew tapped the papers with his finger—"Richard bought into the Dallas thing to the tune of two hundred and fifty thousand dollars. Did Richard have that kind of money?"

I was astounded. "Of course not!" His Porsche, the trips to Europe, clothes, Candace's schools, the house—living well had been an addiction for Richard, his way of making up for having had to work his way through college pumping gas. He could no more have amassed two hundred fifty thousand dollars than he could've allowed himself to wear a poorly cut overcoat.

"He might have borrowed the money," I said weakly.

Andrew nodded. "He might've. If you asked him about it I expect he'd say he did. And your next question should be what he used for collateral. And after that, how's he managing to pay the interest. And you know what you'd find out, if you got him to tell the truth? That he put up nothing, that he's paying nothing, that he's in this project for two hundred fifty g's and he didn't spend a damn dime."

It was storming outside. A gust of wind rattled the windowpanes. A. J. jumped heavily down from his perch and padded out of the room. "I don't understand what you're saying."

"This is the scenario. The Dallas people let Richard in on their deal to the tune of two hundred fifty thousand. The plan is to build the park fast, get the tenants in, and in three years, sell it. Richard gets out with his original 'investment,' which he never made, plus profits."

Andrew was speaking in a well-modulated tone, but somehow I felt as if he were shouting. "I'm saying that was no loan," he continued. "Richard was bribed."

How ugly. What a very ugly syllable the word *bribe* was. It conjured up paper bags filled with money, sleazy back-alley meetings. But of course it didn't have to be that. It could be industrial parks in Dallas, and large unsecured loans, and people who minded their manners and belonged to the Yacht Club. "Bribed to do what?"

"There are lots of ways Richard could help Basic Development. He could give them a five-minute head start on the Golden State Center bidding, so they could come in low. He could talk up Golden State with his cronies on the Redevelopment Commission and the Board of Supervisors so Basic would get their permits fast. He could square them with Public Works so they didn't have any trouble with utility hookups. Richard could do plenty. He's a guy with a lot of juice."

I had lived with Richard, slept with him, thought him handsome, elegant, knowledgeable. Instead, he was just "a guy with a lot of juice" who was willing to sell out. I stared at the disorderly pile of papers. I felt sick.

There was another point—a point Andrew and I hadn't yet discussed. I had found the folder in Richard's safe. He had almost certainly taken it from Larry's office the night Larry died. The idea that Richard might have pushed Larry out the window was no longer particularly farfetched.

"What are you thinking?"

Andrew's hand was on my shoulder. At first, I couldn't speak. Then I blurted out, "I was wondering if Richard killed Larry."

"All we can say is that it looks more likely now." Andrew's matter-of-fact tone made me feel calmer. It wouldn't do, after all, to fly into hysterics because I had discovered that my former husband wasn't only an insensitive philanderer but a criminal, and possibly a murderer as well.

"You're getting green around the gills. Want some wine? I'll get you a nice glass of wine." The anxious offer made little impression on me, aside from a fleeting notion that Andrew was sweet to bother. "Even better," his voice floated from the kitchen, "we didn't have dinner. How about"—the sound of the refrigerator door opening—"let's see. Some scrambled eggs? A salami sandwich?" He reappeared with a water glass half full of red wine. "What do you say?"

I was almost able to smile at his strenuous efforts to resuscitate my spirits. "I love salami."

He looked pleased. "I buy it downstairs. It's the best. Sit right there, and it'll be ready in a second."

Andrew made a very good salami on rye. Washing it down with more rotgut red from the jug on the table between us, I thought how all the elements of my life had moved, changed, taken on a different configuration, like a pile of leaves swirled about by wind. Some leaves fall back, but in a different place. Some blow away forever. At this moment, it was impossible to know what I would keep and what I would lose.

Andrew finished his sandwich and leaned back. While we ate he had barely spoken, perhaps sensing that I preferred not to talk. Now he said, "I've got a question."

"What is it?"

"Do you want to go on with this investigation?"

I had been asking the question of myself. We had reached a watershed. Whatever happened from here on in would be serious. Nothing, I knew, would stop Andrew from going ahead now, but this was my opportunity to bow out, to stay in the background, to be—if possible—safe.

"Yes. I want to go on." Clearly, I couldn't be content with discoveries half-made. I was on my way to finding out what a great deal of my life had been about.

Andrew looked relieved. "I'm glad to hear you say that. A while ago, you got a little—weird. I was afraid you'd changed your mind about Richard. Gotten sympathetic to him, or something."

I shook my head. "I was married to Richard for twenty-two years. I haven't gotten over letting his actions make a difference to me. But sympathetic isn't what I felt."

"Good. Because if you don't mind me saying so, Maggie, you're obviously way too good for that guy. I mean, you're terrific even leaving him out of it. Not a very graceful compliment, but at least I'm sincere."

I was grinning absurdly. "You have a way with words. Have you considered writing as a profession?" The energy that had deserted me came flooding back. "What do we do next?"

"Next, I think we should go to the little place down the street where I always go and make photocopies of this stuff. I've got envelopes and stamps. We'll mail a couple to ourselves, and a couple of others to friends I have who sometimes keep things for me. That way, we won't lose it again. After that, I suggest we join a political protest."

"What kind of protest?"

"Citizens Against the Golden State Center is having a meeting tonight at eight. I'm supposed to cover it. If we hurry, I think we can make it."

SIXTEEN

Andrew was wrong by half an hour. The cigarette smoke was already thick and voices raised by the time we got downtown to the church basement where the meeting was being held. In spite of the terrible weather the room was packed, with most of the audience sitting on folding chairs and the rest leaning against the walls. Damp from the rain and breathless from hurrying to get there, Andrew and I stood at the back, next to a table displaying pamphlets advertising everything from methadone programs to the church's Older Singles group.

In the front of the room a tiny white-haired man, barely

able to see over the podium, was haranguing the crowd. Despite this fact, a steady buzz of conversation came from small knots of people who appeared to be caucusing, and members of the audience got up and wandered at will. The speech seemed to be serving the same function that a cocktail piano serves in a crowded lounge. Andrew took out his notebook, whispered, "He's from the Senior Citizens Lobby," and began scribbling.

The Senior Citizens Lobby spokesman was denouncing the Golden State Center because it would do away with low-cost housing in the neighborhood. "In the words of Richard Longstreet, our esteemed redevelopment director, who was *dreadfully* sorry he couldn't be here tonight to listen to our charges"—the man paused to give the crowd a chance to laugh sarcastically—"as I say, in the words of Mr. Longstreet, the Golden State Center will be 'a part of the neighborhood but also a transformation of the neighborhood—a newborn, vital phoenix rising from underutilized and undervalued land.'"

I squirmed. "I can't believe Richard would say anything that corny," I muttered to Andrew.

He continued to write. "Probably a flight of fancy from his public relations flack."

"—ask you, my friends," the speaker was continuing, "is out of what ashes is Mr. Longstreet's phoenix rising? I submit to you it's from the ashes of the little people who are being displaced because the City Hall fat cats think it's a good idea!"

This shot brought scattered applause and shouts of "Right on!" I thought it would have been a good stopping place, but the speaker made his point several additional times, using phrases like "disregard of the average citizen," "unholy alliance between big business and big labor," and "like to see *them* try to live on Social Security."

I surveyed the crowd. There was no obvious racial or cultural common denominator. "Who are all these people?" I asked Andrew.

His eyes swept the room. "A lot of them probably live around here in cheap hotels that'll be torn down when the Center goes up. Let's see—that group over by the door is the Anti-Highrise Coalition. Very active bunch. I would guess some of the other people are merchants who don't want to sell and move. Hey!" His elbow dug into my ribs. "There's Joseph Corelli!"

"Corelli? Where?"

"Over there. See? Sort of hidden in the corner. Bald, heavyset guy."

The man Andrew described was leaning against the wall, arms folded. He looked like a prosperous businessman in his fifties who had sampled a little more Luigi's pasta than was absolutely necessary. He was wearing a dark suit, and his fleshy face looked glazed with boredom. I wondered what scandalous secret Larry had known about this apparently upstanding man, something so damning that Corelli would pay to keep it quiet. Corelli's name had been on Richard's calendar, too. What was the connection between them?

The senior citizen finished his speech to moderate applause, and there was a certain amount of milling around while the Anti-Highrise Coalition spokesman tried to find something to lean his numerous charts against. I told Andrew about finding Corelli's name on Richard's calendar and said, "I want to talk with Corelli. What could he possibly be doing here?"

"Beats me. We should try to find out." Andrew glanced around. "They usually have some barely potable coffee in that little niche over there. Want to try some while this guy gets organized?"

As we threaded our way through the crowd, I caught snatches of conversation. People were talking about lawsuits, holding actions, and civil disobedience. Everyone referred to the Golden State Center as the "GSC." Bitter voices flung out the name "Longstreet."

When we had almost reached the coffee urn something

caught my eye. I thought there was a familiar face in a group to my left. I looked again, and stopped still.

Standing about four feet away, not looking at me, was the narrow-faced man who had lurked beside my garage to grab me and warn me to stay away from the *Times*. He was smoking a cigarette. As I stared at him, he turned toward me. His eyes widened when they caught mine, and he turned immediately and moved away into the crowd.

"It's the man! The one from last night!" I cried over my shoulder to Andrew as I took off after him, excusing myself to the various citizens whose toes I was mangling. It would be perfect to catch him in this crowd, and demand what he thought he'd been doing. I'd be surrounded by witnesses if he tried to hurt me.

I heard Andrew say, "What—wait a minute!" as I plunged on. I was gaining ground until a group of Anti-Highrisers, deep in a discussion of quality of life, wandered into my path. By the time I had disentangled myself from them, the man was gone.

"You're a real tiger, aren't you?" Andrew sounded irritated.

It had been a stupid thing to do. "I got carried away. But what on earth could he have been doing here? This whole situation gets stranger all the time."

"Just watch out. I don't want you to get carried away—literally."

"Neither do I." I noticed that one advantage of barging across the room was the fact that I was now considerably closer to Joseph Corelli. "Why don't we rendezvous after the next speech. I want to strike up an acquaintance with Mr. Corelli."

Andrew's response was to roll his eyes upward and wander away. I elbowed my way to Corelli's corner and settled against the wall next to him. After a decent interval of listening to the Anti-Highrise speaker, who had finally gotten his charts propped up, I glanced at Corelli and said, "Good crowd here tonight."

Corelli looked at me. Up close, his face was heavily sensual, with full lips and knowing eyes. He looked me over with languid expertise and apparently decided I'd do to relieve his boredom. "They'll never get anything accomplished if they don't get organized," he said, moving closer to me. His voice was deep, and he smelled of pipe tobacco and wine.

"There doesn't seem to be much structure," I said. Corelli had moved so close it was making me nervous.

"Chickens with their heads cut off," he agreed. "The only good reason for coming here is that occasionally a very attractive woman turns up."

Well, well, well. I had made a hit. "Actually, this is my first time here. I don't understand the issues as well as I should."

Corelli bent over me. "There's not that much to understand. These are just a lot of people who object to getting screwed by the city."

"And what are you? One of those people who object to getting screwed?"

He smiled wickedly. "Only in one sense."

I fiddled with the scarf at my neck. I hadn't engendered this much sexual intensity at a first meeting since an eighty-five-year-old retired board chairman fumbled at the front of my dress under the guise of helping me with my coat at a charity benefit string quartet recital. I wondered if Corelli came on like this with every woman he exchanged words with, or if it was my unique charm at work. "No, really," I protested.

"It's a complicated situation, but basically you're right. I own some property that's needed for the Golden State Center. I don't want to sell. I've come to a couple of meetings to see if an efficient protest group would develop. So far I've been disappointed." His smile deepened. "Surely you find this recital of my troubles boring."

"Not at all. It's fascinating." It was outrageous to play

along with him, but it seemed the only basis for our getting acquainted.

"Aren't you kind to say so." His eyelids looked heavy, his voice was smooth. Did he lick his lips, or was it my imagination? "In that case, why don't we go discuss it over a drink, and leave these windbags to their exercises in futility?"

The last place I wanted to be was alone with this turned-on Joseph Corelli. I tried to sound regretful. "I can't. I'm here with a friend. But I'll tell you what." I put my hand on his arm. "I really am interested in discussing this further. Why don't we get together tomorrow afternoon?"

Corelli looked miffed, and I was afraid he'd turn me down. Hope, however, did not die easily. After a minute he grunted a reluctant "All right," and dug in his pocket for a business card. "Come around to the back," he instructed me. "My office opens on the alley."

I shook his hand, arranged to stop by at two o'clock, and slid back into the crowd.

As we drove home after the meeting Andrew said, "You certainly made a hit with Corelli. Are you sure he didn't drool down your neck?"

I felt smug. "My irresistibility is legend. I'm going to pump him about Richard tomorrow."

When we reached the house, Andrew got out of the car. "I'm coming in with you while you make sure that guy hasn't come back."

"Great." We sprinted through the rain. Wet flowers from the Japanese magnolia had blown onto the front steps. The house looked just as I'd left it, one light burning in the living room.

As Andrew followed me into the entry hall, though, I sensed that something was different, that the peace of the house had been disturbed. I didn't know why I thought so. Everything looked the same. With growing uneasiness, I walked into the living room. There, looking as impeccable as ever, was Richard, sitting in an armchair waiting for me.

SEVENTEEN

Invariably well mannered, Richard stood up when I walked into the room. After raising his eyebrows when he saw Andrew, he focused on me. "I want to talk with you."

My immediate response was a slight drag toward acquiescence, a hangover from twenty-two years of agreement to his requests. Before I could say anything, though, I felt a much more powerful flash of resentment. Was there no limit to Richard's gall? This was my home now, not his, but apparently he felt perfectly justified in invading it. "How the hell did you get in?"

"I kept my key." He looked a trifle shamefaced about it, knowing it hadn't been a sophisticated thing to do.

I held out my hand. "Give it to me. I want it right now."

"I'll give it to you. But first I'd like for us to have a chat." He turned to Andrew with blatant inquiry. Richard had always accomplished a great deal by indirection. He didn't have to tell Andrew that Andrew was unwelcome. The arrogant tilt of his head, the slant of his body did it for him.

Andrew didn't budge, and I had no intention of asking him to leave. I was only beginning to realize how dangerous Richard might be. Still, it was unlikely that he had missed the folder yet, so he didn't know how much trouble he was in. "This is Andrew Baffrey, a friend of mine," I said. On impulse, I added, "He's the editor of the *People's Times*."

Only someone who knew Richard as well as I would have seen the look of shock and fear that hung for an instant in his eyes. It transformed his face for me as thoroughly as if I had seen it suddenly made livid in the glare of lightning. And I felt not dismay, and certainly not pity, but triumph. At last, I thought, at last I have the upper hand. Then his self-control reasserted itself and he turned to Andrew and said, coldly, "How do you do?"

Andrew, standing near the door, nodded gravely. Neither offered to shake hands. Richard turned back to me, his eyes freezing. "I want you to tell me what you're up to, Maggie. I want to know right now."

Bubbles of power were eddying through my veins. I felt invulnerable. "I spent a lot of years doing what you wanted me to do, and look where it got me. You can't exact anything from me anymore, Richard. You deliberately gave up that privilege."

Richard squared off to face me. "First you come to my office and make an irrational scene about being followed. Then I hear that you're running around with my enemies, people who want to ruin me. To put it bluntly, I think you're sick. Furthermore, since what you're doing directly concerns me, I deserve an explanation."

So I was sick. Causing trouble for Richard made me ipso facto unbalanced. "Don't get self-righteous with me. If you're so concerned about what you deserve, then I suggest you deserve to spend time in jail."

He took a step nearer. I felt only exhilaration. "What the hell are you talking about?"

In the background I heard Andrew say, "Maggie, wait—" but I couldn't stop myself. "I'm talking about *you*, Richard," I spat out. "You make a pretense of cultivation, but when it comes right down to it you're a crook. Nothing but a cheap crook."

Although it shouldn't have, the slap surprised me. I was aware only of the impact of the blow at first. Caught off balance, I reeled backward against the liquor cabinet and in an effort to keep from falling swept several crystal cordial glasses to the floor. I heard them shatter at the same time I was aware that Andrew had shouted, "Leave her alone!" and bounded across the room, grabbed Richard, and shoved him away from me.

Richard turned savagely. I had never seen him so out of control. "And you!" he shouted at Andrew. "What do you mean, stirring up trouble this way!"

"He didn't stir anything up! I went to him!" I cried.

My face was starting to sting, and I had to blink tears out of my eyes in order to see Richard and Andrew glaring at each other—Richard's tie crooked, Andrew's navy blue sweater pulled to one side. This encounter was taking on all the aspects of a barroom brawl. It was almost funny, in a totally horrible way. I tried to suppress the giggles that were rising in my throat. If I began to laugh, I might not be able to stop until they carted me away. Swallowing hard, I said, "Richard, get out. Give me the key and get out."

His foray into physical violence had left Richard crestfallen. It was with only a trace of his former arrogance that he said, "We haven't settled anything yet."

"We aren't going to. Not tonight. Get out."

Without another word, Richard detached the house key from his key ring, dropped it on the coffee table, and walked out, straightening his tie as he went. After the door clicked, Andrew and I looked at each other. I was still slumped against the liquor cabinet, my hand against my smarting cheek. "Has he hit you often?" Andrew asked.

I shook my head, as much to clear it as in denial. "Never."

"He's a real bastard," he said hotly. "Worse than I thought."

"Rotten. He's absolutely rotten." Without any warning at all, my face was wet with tears. I bent my head and let them flow. Once they had started, I knew there was nothing I could do to stop them. The terror, the anger, the shocks of discovery I had experienced today were sliding out of my eyes and dripping off my chin onto the pretty silk scarf I had put on to take Candace to brunch so many hours ago.

"Maggie." I could feel Andrew's breath on the top of my head. His warm hand was at the back of my neck, guiding me to rest against him. My cheek rubbed the damp, scratchy wool of his sweater. It was so long since I had been offered any physical comfort that I gave myself up to it as I might've submerged myself in a hot bath. Andrew's hand slid across my shoulders. "It's all right," he murmured.

The tears didn't stop for a long time. As it became damper, the front of Andrew's sweater got even scratchier, but the sensation was somehow reassuring. After a few minutes, I put my arms around him. He was so thin. I could have counted the knobs on his backbone. His beard brushed my face when he leaned down to kiss my forehead. Then he kissed my eyes and said, "Salty. You taste like a pretzel."

"What outrageous flattery." I knew for sure that I wanted to go to bed with him. "I never kissed a man with a beard before, except when I was a little girl there was my Great-Uncle Clyde—"

The story of Great-Uncle Clyde was interrupted. Other things were more urgent, and more diverting. It wasn't until much later, when I was drifting off to sleep, that I thought about Uncle Clyde again. "He owned an avocado grove," I said.

"Who?" Andrew yawned widely and settled down against me.

"Uncle Clyde. He had a bushy white beard, and he used to give me avocados."

"Um."

"So that's when I decided beards were nice, probably. Don't you suppose?"

I didn't get Andrew's opinion on the subject, because he was already sound asleep. Very soon afterward, so was I.

EIGHTEEN

Andrew's hair, sticking out at wild angles from deep in the pillow, was the first thing I saw when I woke. It looked like a dense thicket in the field of yellow buttercups printed on the pillowcase. I lay listening to his breathing and thinking over the situation.

What I had done was appalling. I had fallen into bed with a boy twenty years my junior who had sweet-talked me by telling me I tasted like a pretzel. Suppose—I shuddered, but not violently enough to wake Andrew—suppose Candace had chosen *this* morning to visit, instead of yesterday. The very thought put me in an altered state of consciousness.

Andrew sighed and burrowed deeper into his pillow. My God. I was twenty years older. I was old enough to be his mother—his actual, biological mother. Maybe I was only nineteen years older, but still. I ran through all the people I knew and pictured their reactions if they could see me now. The reaction of every single one would be the same. Appalled.

If I *had* to have a tumble in the hay with a schoolboy, I could've at least chosen a clean-shaven one with a nice haircut and some decent clothes. Sure. I could've at least chosen a schoolboy version of Richard.

Andrew's sweater was wadded on the floor beside the bed. I reached down and touched it. It was still a little damp from last night's rain and, for all I knew, from my tears. Feeling it under my fingers, I was overwhelmed with tenderness for Andrew. He had been an attentive lover, had acted thrilled and delighted to be with me. The honest truth was that it had been a lot of fun. And even I, Maggie Longstreet, might be entitled to some fun, albeit under irregular circumstances.

It was appalling, certainly. On the other hand, I probably could have found worse things to do. Perhaps it was an appalling act I could live with. Didn't Colette write a novel about something like this? And look at Edith Piaf. Didn't Edith Piaf—

I felt Andrew nuzzling the back of my neck. "You're awake early," I said.

His breath stirred my hair. "I'm not exactly awake. Only part of me is."

Appalling, but here we were. "You young bucks are insatiable."

"Our most endearing characteristic."

I didn't have time to think about it right then, but when I did I'd look up that novel by Colette.

Later, I sat and drank coffee while he scrambled the eggs, standing at the stove wearing only his jeans. The sunlight fell through the window on his tousled hair, picked out the planes of his neck and his pale shoulders. "The secret is a pinch of oregano," he said.

"I'll add it to my recipe file."

The eggs were delicious, but we had only half-finished them when the phone rang. Its impolite jangle reminded me of all I had succeeded in forgetting since last night, and I answered with regret.

The woman's voice at the other end of the line was cold and businesslike. "Mrs. Longstreet?"

"Yes?"

"My name is Jane Malone."

An eye-opener for sure. I mouthed "Jane Malone" to Andrew, and motioned him toward the extension in the study. "Yes?" I said again.

"I'm with the Basic Development Corporation. I'd like

to talk with you. Would it be possible for you to meet me today?"

I didn't relish getting together with the owner of that voice. "Fine. Shall I come to your office?"

"I'm working at home. The Barbary Plaza. Do you know where it is?"

Know where it is? Did Jane Malone think I could have missed seeing the worst glass-and-concrete eyesore ever to be inflicted on San Francisco's waterfront? "I'm familiar with it." We arranged to meet in an hour and hung up.

"I wonder what she wants," Andrew mused as we finished our eggs. "Listen"—there was concern in his eyes—"you be especially careful. We already know Jane Malone has a lot at stake here."

"I don't think she'll have me garroted in the Barbary Plaza. Wonder why she wants to see me there, anyway, instead of in her office."

"Keeping it unofficial," Andrew said. "Listen. About being careful. I'm not kidding."

The rain had washed the city and left behind it brilliant sun, a dancing wind, and choppy green waves on the bay. By the time I reached the Barbary Plaza, though, my mood was not as bright as the weather warranted, and I felt considerably less confident than when I'd been boasting cozily in my kitchen.

All I knew about Jane Malone was that she was dishonest, had an unpleasant voice, and was known as a difficult customer. "I never saw her in the flesh, but she has a reputation as one tough lady," Andrew had told me before we parted. "She started at Basic as some low-level employee and blasted her way to the top. Nobody ever implies that she screwed her way up, either. From what I hear, she loves making a buck better than anything else. Never been married, or even had a lover, male or female, that anybody knows about."

A tough lady with a taste for the good life, I thought, as I walked between the clipped hedges toward the scarlet-uniformed doorman. The Barbary Plaza had *nouveau riche* written all over it—it was somewhere for rock musicians and drug dealers to stay when they weren't at their places in Marin, or a haven for filty rich entrepreneurs in the human-potential business. The security officer in the two-story lobby took my name and called Jane Malone. Waiting for clearance, I gazed through the glass wall at the terraced gardens in back of the building and the glittering bay beyond. It could be, I thought morosely, that Jane Malone had killer Dobermans. Or that a man with a gun would be hiding behind her door.

In fact, as soon as I rang her bell I heard dogs, but their yapping wouldn't make anybody's blood freeze. Chihuahuas, evidently. When she opened the door two of them, one dressed in a pink knitted sweater and one in a blue, barked insanely at my ankles, prompting me to wonder whether the SPCA would mind my kicking them in their bulging sides.

"Lambie! Gigi! Stop it this minute!" Jane Malone commanded. Then, to me, "Come in, Mrs. Longstreet. They won't hurt you."

I edged into the room, eyeing her curiously. The quintessential tough lady doted on a pair of Chihuahuas? Looking at her, it was hard to believe she ever doted on anything. She was short, stocky, freckled, and she looked as vulnerable as a roll of barbed wire. Her graying reddish hair was short and straight, her broad face devoid of makeup, and her eyes the color of freshly poured concrete. The green pantsuit she wore, while obviously expensive, did nothing to deemphasize the square solidity of her figure.

"Sit down, Mrs. Longstreet." Peremptory tone. Still pursued by Lambie and Gigi, I settled gingerly on the edge of a dark rose brocade chair and looked around. The room was almost a parody of "feminine" bad taste. White shag carpet, rose-and-green antique sofa and chairs, crystal chandelier, two Dresden shepherdesses on the mantelpiece.

Through an open door, I could see the corner of a bed covered with a pink satin bedspread. Looking at Jane Malone again, I saw masses of inner conflict—the hard-nosed businesswoman versus the chatelaine of a fluffy, extravagant boudoir that she shared with two yapping, spoiled, overfed babies.

"Coffee?" The silver service was on the table, with its tiny sugar cubes with tongs for serving them and delicate, flower-decorated china cups. I was certainly getting the treatment. I wondered how long I would have to put up with polite mouthings before I found out what she wanted.

Not long. Jane sipped her coffee once and said, "I understand you attended a meeting of Citizens Against the Golden State Center last night."

Privacy was apparently a meaningless concept these days. "That's right."

"I wonder if you realize that your presence at gatherings such as that one is—how shall I put it—a potential source of embarrassment for Basic Development?"

"I've never thought about it." I had no desire to be anything but brusque with her.

"Possibly you haven't." An excuse for a smile touched her lips. "Let me explain. If you, as the redevelopment director's ex-wife, joined a protest group and became active, and if the media got wind of it—well, you know what the media in this town are like." Her smile deepened. We were buddies, equal in our superiority to the media. "It would be publicity we neither want nor need. Do you understand?"

"I suppose so."

"The point is this." Jane's tone was becoming increasingly mellifluous as mine got more brittle. "I wouldn't ask you to compromise your convictions. But I do want you to know that we would strongly prefer your not joining the protest."

"I see." She obviously expected a further response, but

to hell with her. I sat woodenly, staring at a sentimental nineteenth-century landscape on the opposite wall.

After a few moments she poured more coffee and said, "Mrs. Longstreet, now that you have . . . time on your hands, have you considered getting a job? Part-time, perhaps? A lot of women are doing that these days."

I was surprised at the change of subject. "I suppose I've thought about it, but I don't really have any marketable skills, and jobs are hard to find."

"That's true." Jane seemed lost in contemplation. Then she brightened. "You know, it's funny I thought of it. We have something opening up in public relations that you might enjoy. Writing and research. And actually, the money's quite good for part-time." She sipped delicately and patted her lips with an embroidered napkin. "If you're at all interested, I can alert our personnel department."

I stared at her. So this was how it was done. This was probably how they bought Richard—during a polite conversation over the coffee cups, with suggestions so delicately put they almost didn't sound like a bribe at all. Well, I wasn't Richard, and Jane Malone was waving her fancy job offers at the wrong member of the unemployed.

"No, thank you." I was surprised that I sounded so cool. I stood up. "I have to go now."

Jane's fresh-concrete eyes hardened a little, and she held up a freckled hand. "Wait a moment. If you aren't interested in the job, fine. But I insist that you stay out of the Golden State Center protest. It will be best for everyone if you do. Best for us, and—I'm trying to make this absolutely clear, Mrs. Longstreet—best for you."

Enough was enough. "If that's a threat, then perhaps I should report you to the police. They might want to know where to look if anything happens to me."

"Certainly they might." Jane glanced at a gilded clock. "That reminds me. I'm having drinks with the commissioner later this afternoon."

I wanted to feel my fingers around her squatty neck.

"Have a wonderful time. Enjoy it, before something comes along that even your friend the commissioner can't ignore."

Jane was on her feet, too. "You force me to warn you, Mrs. Longstreet—" she began, but I didn't want to listen to her anymore. I strode to the door and walked out, leaving her to make her threats to Lambie and Gigi.

I was too mad to be frightened until I reached my car, but once there I began to shake. Jane Malone had a lot of clout, and I had made her angry. And if she and Richard were upset now, wait until he discovered the folder was missing. Then they'd really be running scared.

In the midst of these disturbing thoughts I remembered my appointment with Joseph Corelli. It was still early. I drove to Columbus Avenue and, for want of a better alternative, parked in a lot. I wasn't far from Andrew's apartment. I felt an unexpected rush of longing for him, but I knew he'd be at the *Times*. North Beach was looking charming, and bohemian, and all the things it could be if you ignored the Broadway sleaze. A couple of blocks down, Luigi's red and white awning flapped cheerfully. Loath to eat there after Andrew's tale of the violated restaurant code, I went instead to a health-food bar and ate an avocado-and-sprouts sandwich and drank a yogurt shake. My stomach wasn't especially pleased with this intrusion swallowed on top of Jane Malone's threats, and it was with a certain queasiness that I walked down the street to Luigi's.

The lunch rush was over. Outside on the terrace, under a Cinzano umbrella, three old men sat over a carafe of red wine. As Corelli had instructed me, I walked around to the back of the building. The alley was cleaner than most, and looked like a little brick-paved street. The door that must lead to Corelli's office was painted mustard yellow, and was standing slightly ajar.

Left it open for me, I thought, knocking lightly. When there was no response, I stepped inside. Opening onto a short hallway was a no-nonsense office with a desk, filing cabinets, a sofa, and a chair, and it was empty. I thought perhaps Corelli had gone into the other part of the building.

As I turned back to the hall, I saw something shiny by the side of the desk. When I looked more closely, I saw it was the toe of a well-polished shoe.

I moved toward the desk. It was a shoe, and a trouser leg—trousers such as a successful restaurateur might wear. It was, in fact—my queasiness abruptly got worse—Corelli, lying on his side, his eyes staring. His face had none of the avid sensuality of the night before, and his hands clutched his stomach as if he had indigestion. It wasn't indigestion, though, but something much worse. Blood had poured from his shirt front and drenched his hands. A nightmarish puddle of it lay in front of him, soaking into the carpet. In the midst of it all, he stared straight ahead, and I didn't see him blink once.

NINETEEN

The air in the phone booth was stale. Through the grease-smeared glass I could see the red and white awning of Luigi's and the three old men still lingering over their wine. Swallowing compulsively, I leafed through the ragged directory, forgetting for the moment what I was looking for—the number of the police.

I had been unable to stay in the room with Joseph Corelli—or, more precisely, Joseph Corelli's body. Nothing in my life had prepared me for his fixed stare and bloody shirt front. Motion makes the difference, I told myself, and there was no motion left in Corelli. Not in his full, gaping lips, or his bulging eyes, not even in the blood gleaming so stickily where it had gushed through his hands. I had stared at him for a few moments, a peculiar scalding sensation inside me, and then bolted out of the room and down the still-deserted alley.

Once outside, I began to consider what to do. Someone would have to be told. The police would have to be told. I couldn't leave Joseph Corelli lying in his blood on his office floor. It was no good assuring myself that someone would find him eventually. He had been found, and it was my responsibility.

By the time I sagged into the phone booth, my mind was numb. The memory of Corelli's body was already taking on an eerie unreality. Of course *Police Emergency* would be in the front of the book, you idiot. I picked up the receiver.

The voice on the other end of the line sounded interested in my news, if not unduly surprised, and hung up after taking my name and assuring me someone would be there immediately. Next, I fumbled through the phone book again, dropped a dime in the slot, and dialed the *Times*. A young man answered and said Andrew wasn't around, maybe he was at lunch. No, he didn't know when Andrew might be back. I hung up, but clung to the receiver until it was coated with sweat from my hand. God damn.

The police would be arriving any second, and I had to go back to Luigi's. I walked slowly, concentrating on the sidewalk, thinking about how much I should tell them. Jane Malone had unnerved me with her talk about drinks with the commissioner. If I brought in Larry and his blackmail of Corelli, I'd also have to bring in Andrew and the *Times*. I couldn't do that, I could not, without talking to Andrew first. All right. I couldn't do it, so I wouldn't. I reached Luigi's and sat at one of the outside tables under an umbrella to wait for the police.

A lot of them arrived very soon. Within ten minutes the CLOSED sign was swaying on the front door, the scared-looking staff, the three old wine-drinkers, and I were sitting inside at thickly varnished tables littered with pizza crumbs, and Inspector Fred Bosworth was offering me coffee.

Inspector Bosworth displayed little detective glamour. His paunch, thin graying hair, shapeless rust-brown sport jacket and baggy slacks seemed to me more suited to a seedy real-estate salesman than to a dauntless investigator. He looked tired and unshaven, and there was a spot of something dark red—tomato soup, I hoped—on his tie. I tried to avoid looking at it, and, since I was also having trouble looking him in the eye, I found myself staring mostly at my coffee cup.

"Are you all right, Mrs. Longstreet?"

"I think so."

Bosworth clicked his ballpoint pen. "Can you tell me what happened?"

By that time, I had gone over the story repeatedly in my mind, and I ran through it without stumbling. I had met Corelli last night at the Citizens Against the Golden State Center meeting (did Bosworth's eyebrows go up at that?). He had offered to fill me in on some of the issues, and we had made an appointment to meet today. When I arrived, I found his body. I had seen no one enter or leave Corelli's office. It was simple, straightforward, and true—as far as it went—and Bosworth seemed satisfied. He told me I could go, and as I gathered my coat and purse he scratched his stubbly cheeks with the button end of his ballpoint and said, "You any relation to Redevelopment Director Longstreet?"

"Not any more," I said stiffly. "I used to be married to him."

"Uh-huh." Bosworth wrote something in his notebook and studied it closely, as if it had been rendered indecipherable. "Think the Golden State Center is a bad deal?" he asked conversationally.

"I haven't made up my mind yet. I like to get all sides of the story."

Surely the tremor in my voice would make Bosworth suspicious, but apparently tremors were all in a day's work for him. He merely closed his notebook, thanked me, and told me to come by the station to sign my statement. He appreciated my cooperation. His eyes looked as if he had already forgotten me.

I left Luigi's in a daze. The wind had picked up, and my coat was no longer warm enough. I pulled it closer and hurried toward the parking lot. I wanted to see Andrew, and the sooner the better.

I found him in the *Times* newsroom, deep in a discussion with two other people about somebody butchering somebody else's copy. When he saw me he disengaged himself, smiling. "You're here! What a terrific surprise."

I couldn't smile back. "I have news."

We went into his office, and I managed to tell the story relatively calmly, finishing with, "I tried to call you, but they told me you were at lunch."

"Yeah, I had to get out. This place is a real pressure cooker." He leaned against the windowframe, his face grim. "We're in deep trouble. You know as well as I do that all this is tied up together."

"I know. I just don't know what to do about it."

He was silent a long time, gazing out the window. As I looked at him, my mind escaped from current stresses by appreciating how gorgeous he was. Gorgeous knobby wrists, unruly hair, well-worn running shoes. Gorgeous faded jeans, brown eyes—

"Maybe it's time we went to the police," he said.

"You mean tell them everything?"

He was pale. "Yeah. Let them handle Richard, Jane Malone, Corelli, Larry, the whole can of worms. What do you say?"

I had expected him to fight ferociously against such an idea, although it seemed obvious to me that it was the only sensible move. Now that he had suggested it himself, I was surprisingly reluctant. I told him what Jane Malone had said about having drinks with the commissioner. "We should tell them, but I'm afraid they'll find excuses for not doing anything. Then we'll have tipped our hand and we'll be left unprotected."

"Yeah. Shit."

Neither of us said anything. I realized I was clenching my hands together so tightly my fingers ached. Finally, I spoke. "I think we should go to the police. But there are a couple of things I'd like to do first."

"What?"

I wasn't sure how he'd take what I was going to say. "I'd like to tell Susanna Hawkins what's going on. Not about the Corelli part, the blackmail part. Just that we suspect everything isn't right about Larry's death. I've been the left-out wife, and I know it isn't pleasant. I'd rather not leave it to a policeman knocking on her door."

"Sure."

"OK. I'll call, and see if she's home this afternoon."

"What else?"

This one would be more difficult. "I'd like for the two of us to have a talk with Richard."

Andrew's expression didn't change. He folded his arms across his chest. "Why?"

"We've got the bribery proof against him. Nothing can change that. But before we involve him in a murder investigation I'd like to hear what he has to say about how that folder got into his safe." When Andrew didn't answer immediately, I went on, "It seems fair."

"And obviously, we'd want to be fair to Richard." His tone was heavy with sarcasm.

I stood up. "I'm sorry you're taking that attitude."

"Come on. Don't get haughty." He approached me and put his hands on my shoulders. Looking into my eyes, he said, "I'm afraid you're pulling both ways on this thing."

Although I knew the answer, I said, "What do you mean?"

"Now that push has come to shove, you're having second thoughts about turning Richard in, aren't you?"

It was a reasonable question. "Not about the bribery

thing. And if I'm convinced he killed Larry I won't hesitate about that, either. I want to hear his story about the night of Larry's death, that's all." I hesitated, then said, "Believe me."

We looked into each other's eyes for a moment before he released me and said, "Oh, hell. All right. Do you think you can get something set up for tonight?"

"Richard said he wanted to talk. I expect he'll jump at the chance."

In fact, my call to Richard was put through with unprecedented speed—so fast I didn't have time to prepare for the lurch of fury I felt when I heard his voice. Here I was, trying to act decently toward a man who had slapped my face. My cheek tingled at the memory, and only an effort of will enabled me to extend my offer of a conversation.

Richard accepted with what was, for him, pathetic eagerness, even to the point of agreeing to Andrew's presence without a murmur. "Shall I come to the house?"

"Absolutely not."

"Why don't we make it for dinner, then? I can get a private room at Arturo's."

Richard's maxim was, never miss a chance to dine in a place that gets mentioned in the columns. "That'll be fine. We'll meet you there at seven-thirty."

As I was about to hang up he said, "Maggie . . ."

"Yes?"

"I want to apologize for hitting you last night. I know it was unforgivable, but—"

"You're right, Richard. It *was* unforgivable," I said, and hung up.

I sat at the phone a few minutes, then picked it up again to dial Susanna Hawkins.

TWENTY

Two teenage boys wearing leather mitts were tossing a baseball back and forth across Barton Street while younger children screamed and chased one another along the sidewalk. In the deepening twilight, the Hawkins house didn't look quite as shabby as it had before. Susanna had readily agreed to see me when I called, and the porch light was on. Curly, the white sheepdog, was sitting on the front steps. He yawned as I walked past him and rang the doorbell.

Susanna was wearing a blue sweater and a long, light green skirt printed with blue flowers. Her face seemed thinner than when I had last seen her, with hollows under the cheekbones. Her hair, straight and shining, fell over her shoulders and down her back like a brown silk shawl. September Apple's remark about Larry came back to me. *Having a lot of women was a big macho thing for him*. It would be easy to wonder why a woman as stunning as Susanna wasn't enough for Larry, but all sorts of things went on between husbands and wives—or didn't go on. I was past thinking beauty, or good intentions, or even sainthood could make a marriage work, and far past trying to figure out what could.

"The boys are playing next door, so I'm not quite as frantic as I was," she said, ushering me in. "How's your article coming?"

I removed a toy truck from a chair and sat down. "That's what I want to talk with you about."

"You need more help?"

"No. There isn't any article." Her face was clouding, and I decided to get it all out at once. "I came to tell you that Andrew Baffrey and I have been looking into it, and we think there was something suspicious about Larry's death."

It had been a mistake to blurt it out like that. Susanna's face blanched, and she shook her head as if her neck muscles had gone out of control. Shocked at the vehemence of her reaction and afraid of a bout of hysterics like the one she'd had at the *Times*, I stood, thinking I'd get water. "I apologize. I'm afraid I'm handling this badly," I gabbled.

She held up a hand to stop me from leaving. "Are you from the police?" she whispered.

"No, no I'm not." I strove for heartiness, to reassure her. "My name is Maggie Longstreet. My former husband is Richard Longstreet, the redevelopment director. Andrew and I have reason to believe Richard might have been involved in Larry's death."

She stared at me, her throat contracting. I felt horrible. At last she said, "Why would your ex-husband want to kill Larry?"

"Larry had information that would cause trouble for Richard. He was going to publish it. We know that Richard took the information from Larry's office the night Larry died."

"Oh." She leaned back and closed her eyes. When she opened them she said, "But what about the note?"

"I saw—couldn't help seeing the note the day you were at the *Times* office. He didn't really say he was going to kill himself, just that he was sorry . . ." I stopped, embarrassed. Sorry for what? What had he been planning, if not suicide?

"Yeah," she said softly. The color was beginning to return to her face. "This is such a shock that I'm acting dumb," she said. "I think I'd like to fix some tea."

I trailed her to the kitchen protesting that she shouldn't, but she insisted on putting the water on to boil. I sat at the kitchen table, looking at the discolored sink and the worn linoleum. The kitchen window had a view of the small backyard, where bright plastic toys lying in the grass were still discernible through the dusk.

"What do you plan to do now?" she asked, spooning lemon grass into a brown pot.

"We're having a talk with Richard tonight. After that, I suppose we'll go to the police. Unless Richard has an explanation, of course."

She poured the steaming water into the pot. "What sort of explanation could he possibly give?"

"I don't know."

She sat at the table, leaning her cheek against one hand, gazing out the window. "Look at those toys out there in the damp. I ask the boys to bring them in, but they forget." She sighed, and looked back at me. "So you're divorced?"

"Recently."

"You have kids?"

"A daughter at Stanford."

"She's grown up. When you have little kids—" She broke off and got up to pour the tea. After a minute, she said, "I'm still in shock about what you've told me. I wish I could think of something to say, but I can't. It's a total surprise."

"I thought you should know."

"You're right. I should." She put a mug in front of me and sat down again. "It seems so strange."

"It does to me, too."

The scent of the lemon grass hung in the air. We drank in silence until she said, "I almost forgot. Did you say you were working with Andrew?"

"Yes."

"There's an envelope of stuff I'd like you to give him for me. I found it in our safe-deposit box—Larry's and mine—but it must belong at the *Times*, because it doesn't mean anything to me." She got up and went into another room, and I heard a drawer open and close. "It's about a man named Joseph Corelli."

My hand jerked, sending tea slopping over the side of my mug. This had to be the information Larry had used to blackmail Corelli. I was mopping the table with a paper towel when Susanna returned and handed me a fat manila envelope with "Corelli" written on it in Larry's hand. "It looks like a story Larry wrote and decided not to use. An exposé about the man who owns those Luigi places. I thought Andrew should have it."

I tried not to grab the envelope too avidly. "I'll be sure he gets it. I'm going to see him right now." Getting up and edging toward the door, I mumbled thanks for the tea.

"Can we talk again when I've thought about what you told me?" she asked as we said good-bye. Assuring her that we could, I escaped with the envelope pinned under my arm.

Once in the car, I was torn between opening it then and there or waiting until I got back to the *Times*. I compromised by taking a quick peek. Among other documents, the envelope contained a sheaf of fifteen-year-old clippings from a Vermont newspaper giving a day-by-day account of the trial of a restaurant owner for criminal negligence in a case of mass food poisoning. Two people had died, and more than twenty patrons of the restaurant had been seriously ill. The owner, a man named Luchese, usually held a coat over his head when he was in camera range. One photo, however, printed under the headline GUILTY VERDICT IN POISONING CASE, showed a thinner, hairier Joseph Corelli hurrying down a flight of steps surrounded by police guards.

It was easy to figure out now. Luchese-Corelli had served a prison term, changed his name, and come to San Francisco to reestablish himself (and continue, apparently, his careless habits of food preparation), only to find himself in danger of being exposed as a mass poisoner. Once that news got out, Luigi's Pasta Palazzos would be finished and Corelli would be down the drain once again. I closed the envelope and started the car. Andrew was going to be excited when he saw this.

TWENTY-ONE

Betsy wasn't at her desk, and I was rushing through her office toward the newsroom, intent on showing the envelope and its contents to Andrew, when I was arrested by a voice calling, "Hey!"

I skidded to a stop. I hadn't noticed September Apple sitting in the far corner, bent over a small table. In front of her were several file boxes filled with three-by-five cards, and piles of cards were scattered over the table. Her pudgy face, streaked with tears and grime when I last saw her, was cleaner now, her dark hair less tousled. She frowned at me. "I know you, don't I?"

I hated to wait, but I was curious about how September was doing. "I'm Maggie Longstreet. I gave you a ride home, remember?"

She looked confused. "Longstreet? A ride home?" Then comprehension dawned. "Oh, yeah. When I was strung out over Larry." She gestured at the cards in front of her. "I'm working for Betsy. Straightening out the subscription list."

I suspected it was a more appropriate job for September than writing articles about the poetry scene. "That's wonderful." I backed up a step. "I've got to—"

"Larry used to talk about a guy named Longstreet," she said.

I stopped. "He did?"

"Sure. Richard Longstreet. He a relative of yours?"

"My ex-husband."

"Oh." That question settled, September went back to arranging the cards.

Instead of rushing off to look for Andrew, I took a step toward her. "What did Larry say about Richard?"

She nibbled the corner of a card, regarding me warily. "I don't know if I should say. Larry made a big deal that anything he said to me was private. If this Richard Longstreet ever found out—"

"I won't tell him. I promise." I'd even cross my heart, if she wanted me to.

"Well—OK, then." She'd been easy to convince. I sensed that talking about Larry, no matter what the excuse, was a release for her. "He never said anything very specific. For a while, he went on about how he was on Longstreet's trail, he was going to get him. Then one day, I remember he came over and he was flying. He was higher than a kite, and I know he hadn't taken anything, because he never did. I remember it so well."

Her voice was soft, and she gazed vacantly in front of her. "He said, 'September, I've got Longstreet. I've got him by the nuts. All I have to do is squeeze.' And the look in his eyes, you wouldn't have believed. I'll tell you, he was getting off on the idea of squeezing this Longstreet's nuts. I was a little spooked."

So was I. "Did he ever say anything else?"

"After that he sort of quit talking about Longstreet, except for one time. He was chuckling to himself and I asked why, and he said, 'Longstreet is running scared. The idiot is even threatening me with violence.' Then he said something like, 'When this story hits the street, you'll hear him yell from here to LA.'" She shrugged. "That was about it."

It was plenty. Richard had threatened Larry with violence. Richard had known Larry was on to him, and he was terrified. Chilled, both at Richard's terror and Larry's sadism, I turned once again toward the newsroom.

The conversation with September didn't dampen my

pleasure in seeing Andrew's eyes goggle when I said, "Susanna sent you this," and dropped the Corelli envelope on the desk in front of him. His reaction was all I could've hoped. After a cursory examination of the clippings and a story outline the envelope also contained, he pounded his fist on the desk in glee. "This is it!" he exulted. "No wonder Corelli was willing to pay through the nose!" He jumped up and stuck his head out the office door. "Hey, Judith!" he yelled. "Kill all that Board of Supervisors analysis! We're redoing the front page!"

"Fuck yourself, Baffrey!" a female voice yelled back.

"I'm *serious*!" He turned back to me, his eyes shining. "The paper comes out tomorrow, so we can get the jump on the dailies. They're going to look sick." He flipped back through the envelope's contents. "Yeah. It's all here."

It was like watching a six-year-old with a new set of Tinkertoys. "Shouldn't you give it to the police?"

"Oh yeah, yeah. *After* our story is written. Better make a copy." As he dashed from the room the female voice cried, "Are you *crazy*, Baffrey?"

He was back in a few minutes, clutching originals in one hand, copies in the other. He dropped them on the desk and said, "Jesus, I don't know how we'll ever make the deadline." He turned toward the door and roared, "Hey, Judith! Come *on*!" Grasping my elbow, he said, "Maggie, this is outstanding. This story coupled with Corelli's murder is going to be dynamite. Plus, we can get into the licensing process, how did a convicted poisoner get a license to run a restaurant in San Francisco, the Luigi's health code violations, do we need more safeguards, all that. It'll be *great*."

Clearly, Andrew wouldn't want to discuss anything else until he had his story on track. I arranged to meet him at Arturo's at seven-thirty and left him in excited consultation with Judith.

I was trying to fight it, but on the drive home I admitted to myself that I felt melancholy and left out. Andrew had the *Times* to think about, and that was something positive, creative. I had only the wreck of my own and other people's lives.

I was passing Pacific Bakery Mall, one of Richard's pet projects. It was a former sourdough bread bakery that, when the original firm sought lower rents in South San Francisco, was rescued from unsightly vacancy and incipient decay by being transformed into a shopping mall. Richard had given a speech on opening day. "All this," he had said, gazing around him at the wine bars, boutiques selling unbleached cotton clothing from Greece, and T-shirt emporia, "all this in a space that for years had only minimal utilization." Maybe my life had had only minimal utilization, too.

By the time I got home I was thoroughly out of sorts. I flung off my clothes and took a long, hot shower. Afterward, as the steam cleared from the bathroom mirror, I looked at myself.

I was surprised. It could have been the residue of dampness on the glass, but in fact I didn't look too bad. Green eyes, chestnut hair, the odd wrinkle to add character. Maggie Longstreet at forty-four. It could be possible, couldn't it, that I might still hope for more than minimal utilization? At least I was still here and still kicking. Somewhat cheered, I began thinking about what to wear to dinner.

Black would strike the right note of severity. I donned a dress I hadn't worn since the funeral of a member of the mayor's staff who collapsed and died of a heart attack in the apartment of a notorious "sex therapist," to the consternation of his wife and six children. Tonight was certainly at least as solemn an occasion, I thought, attaching a diamond-sprinkled pin to my dress at the neck. I pinned my hair up in a French twist. A drop or two of perfume on the pulse points, and I was ready to go. It wouldn't do to keep Richard waiting.

TWENTY-TWO

Arturo's was far enough from the waterfront to escape the tourist trade, but close enough to have been the site of a restaurant, or at least so the story went, since shortly after the Gold Rush. The paneled walls were lined with portraits of famous San Francisco visitors and denizens—Mark Twain, Oscar Wilde, Lola Montes, Robert Louis Stevenson, Alice B. Toklas, Dashiell Hammett, Enrico Caruso—all of whom were rumored to have eaten and rhapsodized over filet of sole Arturo. Whatever the truth of the matter, Arturo's remained one of San Francisco's most prestigious restaurants. It lived up to its legendary status by providing, in addition to excellent food, the whitest table linen, the most lustrously polished woodwork, and the most superannuated and worldly-wise waiters in town.

Giles, the maitre d', was among the oldest, and was certainly the most haughty, of the lot. When I arrived, he inclined his formidable nose and offered to lead me to the private dining room where, despite the fact that I was right on time, Richard was already installed.

The posh little candy box of a room had probably been used for turn-of-the-century (and possibly more recent) dalliances as well as business deals. It was furnished with a roomy, dark-red plush sofa as well as a dining table shining with crystal and silver. A bottle of champagne, Richard's preferred tipple, was cooling in a bucket on a hammered brass stand. Richard stood beside the table, holding a filled glass. When I walked in he nodded cursorily and said, "Where's Baffrey?"

"He'll be here." I hoped the Corelli story wouldn't prove so consuming that he'd forget.

Richard helped me with my coat and poured me a glass of champagne. We could've still been married, waiting for one or another of his business associates to show up with his wife or—more frequently these days—his girlfriend to make up a jolly foursome for an expensive and elegant dinner. The only difference between then and now was the dead silence between us, and come to think of it that wasn't so different either.

Richard cleared his throat. I could see that he was under a strain. His tennis tan had faded, leaving his face washed out and sallow. "Maggie, as long as Baffrey isn't here, maybe I can take this opportunity"—he poured himself more champagne, and his hands were shaking—"this opportunity to ask exactly what you're doing and why. I know you're getting involved with the anti–Golden State Center people—"

"My life seems to be an open book."

"I didn't have to have you followed to find that out. It's difficult to keep these things secret if you're going to attend a public meeting. What I want to know is, why? Is it simply to embarrass me?"

My champagne flute felt cool and fragile in my fingers. As cool and fragile, I thought, as the politeness between Richard and me. "It's because I want to learn the truth about you."

"Learn the truth!" he said impatiently. "I loathe it when people talk that way. Who the hell do you think you are, talking about truth and being so goddam pious?"

I raised my eyebrows. "The evening is running true to form. Did you bring your brass knuckles?"

He flushed and turned away. We were saved from descent into recriminations by Giles, who, with a look easily identifiable as disdain, ushered Andrew into the room.

Despite the strained atmosphere, I had to smile at Andrew. In the midst of his Corelli scoop, he had made an effort to dress for Arturo's, and had discarded his accustomed red nylon windbreaker and navy sweater for a creased green corduroy jacket and a tie in a floral pattern so garish that at any other moment it would have made me laugh aloud. The sartorial revolution hadn't extended below his ankles, however. His blue running shoes were still the footgear of the day.

Andrew seemed as tense as Richard and I, and it was with considerable awkwardness that we managed to order dinner and fill the time until it was served. After the waiter whisked out the door, leaving in front of me a plate of fried calamari I thought I'd die if I had to eat, Richard said, "All right. What do you want to talk about?"

This was a fine moment to realize that Andrew and I hadn't agreed on how to begin. Andrew, contemplating the grilled petrale on his plate, gave no sign of planning to speak in the next hour or two. I decided to plunge in and hope for inspiration along the way. "Richard, perhaps it would be easiest if I told you that Andrew and I know about your financial arrangements with Jane Malone. We know you were paid off to work with Basic Development on the Golden State Center. You don't have to waste time acting outraged."

Richard put down his fork. "You'd better watch your mouth, Maggie. Do you realize how much harm you could do me, talking like that?"

"You said you didn't like to discuss truth. But what I said is the truth. Isn't it?"

Richard's eyes swiveled between Andrew and me, and I could see him trying to think on his feet, work out a story that would put us off.

Andrew said, "We know it's true. We know about the story Larry had on you."

Something changed in Richard's face. He was a pragmatist. I didn't think he would fight for territory that was irrevocably lost, and I was right. He switched his ground, giving up the window dressing of protest. "If you have Larry's story, then you only have Larry's side of it."

"That's right," Andrew said.

Nobody was eating. My throat had closed so tightly I couldn't swallow. Although Richard seemed composed, I saw a drop of perspiration standing at his hairline. He had a look of intense concentration, as if he were playing in a chess tournament, or performing an experiment in ESP.

"Exactly what do you have?" he asked.

"Dallas, Framton Associates, a two-hundred-fifty-thousand-dollar partnership," Andrew answered promptly.

"I see." Richard patted his mouth with his napkin. He looked from me to Andrew and said, "Let me try to explain how it was. I know it will sound naïve, but I actually didn't realize what was happening until it was too late to back out."

He was incredible. I couldn't keep the sarcasm out of my voice when I said, "Surely you're doing yourself an injustice."

He shot me a baleful look. "You don't have to believe me. I'm sure you wouldn't give credence to anything I'd say."

"I only beg you to spare us any tales of being a yokel caught out of your depth. You've spent your whole life making sure you're not one."

He turned to Andrew. "I admit Jane Malone introduced me to Bill Framton. It was a purely social occasion. We met for drinks at the Yacht Club. After that, Bill and I played tennis a few times while he was in town. He's a great player. Wiped up the court with me." He made an attempt at a self-deprecating grin that was almost grotesque. Getting no response, he went on. "He was in town for a couple of weeks, and I saw quite a bit of him. He's not your typical cowboy. Very knowledgeable fellow, knows a lot about art. Collects paintings."

The last was meant to appeal to me. I was supposed to

say, "Oh, really? What artists does he like? What period? How fascinating." I was twisting Arturo's spotless napkin as if it were a dishrag.

"His last night in town we had dinner together," Richard resumed. "Great evening, very enjoyable. After dinner, we were drinking brandy, and he started talking about his latest project—an industrial park in Dallas. Just casual conversation, you know. I was interested, and gave him a few pointers, and before I knew it he had offered me a partnership." Some of the lines in Richard's face smoothed out in the remembered glow of that evening.

"Why didn't you tell him straight out you couldn't afford it?" I asked.

Richard opened his hands wide. "I did. That's exactly what I told him. I said, 'I'm salivating, but I don't have that kind of cash.' I laid it on the line."

"At which point he offered you a loan," Andrew said.

"That's right. He offered me a loan, and I took it because it was too damn good a deal to turn down."

Andrew toyed with his fork. "You didn't think it was odd when he didn't ask for security?"

"Yes," said Richard tightly.

"You didn't wonder what was expected of you for this fabulous deal? Or didn't you know already?" Andrew watched Richard narrowly.

"All right!" Richard threw down his napkin and got up so rapidly his chair fell backward, hitting the floor with a thump. "All right, if you don't want to try to understand how it was. How could I expect a snot-nosed, self-righteous little bastard like you to comprehend anything about business?" He backed away from us. "Yes, I knew what was happening. But you won't make me out to be a criminal. It wasn't done in a—a criminal way."

Neither Andrew nor I said anything. I actually felt embarrassed for Richard. Did he believe that because a bribe had been offered and accepted over after-dinner brandy he was absolved of wrongdoing?

Richard glared at us for a few moments, then sat on the sofa. "Now I want you to tell me something," he said grimly. "Larry Hawkins didn't broadcast the details of stories he was working on, but you've got details. How did you get them? Just how the hell did the two of you find out about this?"

TWENTY-THREE

The atmosphere in the room seemed to vibrate. So far, we'd had only confirmation of what we already knew. Now it was time to explore uncharted territory, and it was my move.

"The fact is, we found the story in a folder—the folder where Larry kept his work in progress," I said. A startled, uncomprehending frown appeared on Richard's face. "And the way we got the folder is interesting. I found it in your safe, Richard. The wall safe in your office. We'd like to know how it happened to be there."

It took Richard a few moments to take in what I'd said. His face blanched whiter beneath the remains of his tan, giving him a jaundiced look. Then his color came flooding back and he said, "You bitch. You'll never give up until you've nailed me to the wall, will you?"

Andrew's hand was on my arm. "Why don't you just explain how you got the folder?" he said.

Richard ignored him and raged at me, "Christ, Maggie, what would it take to get you off my back? You mean to tell me you had the sheer gall to go in my office and ransack my safe—"

"I doubt it took more gall for me to do that than it took

123

for you to get the folder from Larry," I retorted. "He didn't hand it to you for safekeeping, did he?"

Richard stood up. "Why the hell should I tell you?" He moved toward the door.

Andrew pushed his chair back and rose to face Richard. "I'll suggest why you should tell us. You should tell us because you're in a very bad position. The folder disappeared the night Larry died, and it turned up in your safe. Don't you think that needs explaining?"

"Larry committed suicide. That has nothing to do with me."

We were back to Richard and me in the kitchen, the quince preserves, the telephone call. *Sure, I agree Larry Hawkins is a pain in the ass.* . . . "If it has nothing to do with you, how did you know he was going to do it?" I asked. "I heard you say on the telephone that he wouldn't be bothering you much longer. I know you threatened him, too."

Richard looked at me blankly, his stare as fixed as that of a department-store mannequin. He didn't seem to be moving or breathing. At last, he began shaking his head— almost like a shiver at first, then in wider arcs. "Oh, no. Oh, no."

At that moment, the possibilities were infinite. He might attack me, burst into tears, lunge toward the door in an attempt to escape. He did none of those things. He kept looking at me and shaking his head, and finally he choked out, "Are you insane? Are you saying you think I killed Larry Hawkins?"

"We're saying the circumstances are suspicious," Andrew said.

Richard's hands went to his face in an age-old gesture of horror. "You can't believe that. It isn't true."

"If there's an explanation, we want to know what it is," I said.

Richard looked at the door, hesitated, then returned to the sofa and sat down. Andrew slid back into his chair.

Richard's face worked for a moment before he began to speak. "I took the folder from Larry's office. I may as well admit it. I had known for several months that he was working on a story about me. The rumors were flying. In fact, at one point I called him up and demanded to know what was going on. Of course he wouldn't tell me." His voice rose. "He was so offensive I got angry, and told him I'd damn well better not run into him on the street, or I'd personally beat his ass to a pulp. Maybe those are the threats you're talking about."

The conversation was easy to imagine. Richard overbearing, Larry taunting. "After a while, it occurred to me to fight fire with fire," Richard went on. A hint of self-satisfaction asserted itself in his tone, and I could tell he still thought it had been a good idea. "I began investigating Larry. I have a few connections that made it fairly easy to look into the *Times*'s finances." He looked pointedly at Andrew. "You know, Larry wasn't particularly well liked in this town, so his privacy wasn't universally respected."

"No kidding." Andrew didn't sound surprised.

"Anyway, it didn't take long before I realized there were irregularities. Money came in that was unaccounted for. I hope it won't shock you to learn that your precious Larry's hands weren't especially clean. I figured knowing that would give me a fair bargaining position."

So Richard too had uncovered the Corelli blackmail. Larry's number had obviously been up on that scheme. Richard went on, "Once I got on to that, I knew that if worst came to worst I could have a session with Larry and use my information to try to convince him not to publish. I held off, though, because it was my last card, and I didn't want to play it too soon. I expect that's when I said we wouldn't have to worry about Larry much longer. I was probably talking to Jane Malone."

"What about the folder, Richard? What about the night Larry died?" said Andrew evenly.

"I'm getting to that." Richard leaned forward, resting his chin on his clasped hands. "The night of Larry's death was the night I picked to have a showdown with him. The whole subject had been preying on my mind for weeks. I had worked late, and I went out for a few drinks and thought about it, and then, all of a sudden, I couldn't stand it anymore. You know how that can be? One minute a situation is tolerable and the next minute it isn't? So I decided to see if Larry was in his office. Right then. It must've been about eleven o'clock. I suppose I was a little drunk.

"I drove to the *Times*. Maybe I didn't really think he'd be there. When I went by, though, there was a light on up on the seventh floor, so I thought I'd see if I could get into the building. I parked, and the door was unlocked so I went in and took the elevator up. Nobody was around. I found the office with Larry's name pasted on the door and went in. The light was on and the window was open, so I figured he'd just gone out to the can and I decided to wait. When I read the newspaper the next day—I swear that's the first time I realized he must have gone out the window just before I got there."

I didn't look at Andrew. The fact was that I was finding Richard's story quite plausible. Yet what had I expected? That he would break down and confess to murder? Appearances had always been Richard's strong point, and his talents in that direction hadn't deserted him. Naturally, when his need was most desperate he'd call all his resources into play.

"So you're in Larry's office," Andrew said.

Richard nodded. "I stood waiting for Larry to come back, wandering around looking at the books in the bookcase and so on. As I was passing the desk I saw the folder lying on top of a lot of other papers. I wouldn't have looked twice at it, but it was open, and sticking out a little way was a piece of paper that looked like my letterhead. That's what caught my attention.

"You have to admit, the temptation was pretty irresistible." His tone was belligerent. "It was all spread out in front of me. Of course I looked at it."

126

"It shook you up?" Andrew said.

"What the hell do you think? I never imagined he could have so much. I had thought the story was going to be a serious nuisance, not a major disaster." Richard ran his hands over his face, his long fingers pressing for a moment on his eyes. "Then I did a very stupid thing," he continued, almost lightly. "I panicked. All I could think about was getting the information away from Larry. I didn't stop to think that he could reconstruct it, that he'd probably suspect I took it—I didn't consider anything at all. It was like—like being stripped naked in public, and the only way I could get my clothes back on was to take that folder. So I took it."

"And you put it in your safe," I said.

"I thought it wouldn't be disturbed there." Richard shot me a caustic look. "I read through the stuff that night, and it got worse and worse. Of course I realized how irrational it had been to take the folder in the first place, but it was too late. I thought Larry would've come back and missed it by then. I should've gotten rid of it right away, but I wanted to go over it once again and see if I could tighten up any loopholes, figure out how Larry had managed to ferret out his information."

Richard sat back. "That's what happened. I didn't kill Larry. If you still think I did, you're seriously wrong."

Andrew said, "Did anybody see you at the *Times*? Entering or leaving the building, I mean? Or did you see anybody?"

Richard shook his head. "Nobody. Nobody at all."

I felt empty. I had insisted on hearing Richard's story, and now, having heard it, I had learned nothing. Richard was a smooth man, and he had a smooth story. Whether or not he had pushed Larry out the window was as much a mystery to me as ever.

After a short silence Andrew said, "Richard, Maggie and I discussed the situation this afternoon. She wanted to find out what you had to say before we took our information to the police. Now that we've talked—"

"Just a minute," Richard said, with fear in his voice. "You can't take this to the police. You can't. It would ruin me."

"You're ruined already," I said. "A bribery scandal won't get you any medals."

"Christ, yes, that's bad enough," he said wildly. "But not a murder investigation! I did not kill Larry Hawkins. You have to believe me. Please!"

Andrew shook his head. "You can't expect us to ignore this. If you've been telling the truth, you won't have to worry."

Richard made a beseeching gesture, his eyes staring. "No! For God's sake!"

He looked harassed, disheveled—and very small. In that instant, I saw that the compelling, cruel, demonic Richard I had been carrying around with me had shrunk into this craven, frightened, pitiful man. I realized that even if he had killed Larry Hawkins, it would have been from weakness rather than mystical, menacing strength. Richard no longer had a hold on me. It was a separation much more powerful and far-reaching than the physical one had been. At last, we were truly disconnected.

TWENTY-FOUR

I had released Richard, and he tumbled away from me, as light, brittle, and useless as a husk. My ears were filled with a sound like wind, and I listened to it and not to Richard and Andrew, whose lips moved in a pantomime of conversation.

Then Richard held up his hand and the wind-sound in my

ears cleared and I heard Richard say, "Wait. I've just remembered something."

"What is it?" Andrew asked.

Richard spoke slowly. "You asked me if I saw anyone at the *Times* that night. Well, I did."

Andrew raised his eyebrows. "And it's just come back to you now?"

Richard disregarded Andrew's unbelieving tone. "When I was driving past the building, looking up to see if the lights were on, somebody came out the door and walked down the street."

"Did you recognize this person?"

"No. It was dark. And besides"—he chewed his lip for a moment—"whoever it was had on a jacket with a hood. A sheepskin jacket!" He looked at us triumphantly.

"Incredible that you remembered," Andrew said drily.

"Yes, it is. I guess it's because I was going over it so minutely in my mind. But that's the way it happened. I saw a figure in a sheepskin jacket come out of the building and hurry down the street. That's exactly how it was."

It was almost a shame. Richard had been carrying things off so well up to now, only to destroy his credibility with an absurd last-minute concoction. It was like watching an expert tightrope walker take an awkward spill. When neither Andrew nor I responded, he said, "I saw somebody in a sheepskin jacket. I did."

His presence was beginning to oppress me, and I wanted to get away. It seemed that I had been sitting for days in this little room with a plate of cold calamari in front of me, listening to explanations and accusations. The world outside—Giles, the diners who were probably enjoying dinner at Arturo's, the city of San Francisco, the bay, the hills—seemed like an impossible fantasy created by someone whose world was bounded by a champagne bucket and a red plush sofa. I stood up. "Let's go," I said to Andrew.

"Wait a second," Richard said. "What are you going to do?"

I took my coat from the rack. "What we always intended to do."

He was close beside me. "You expect me to stand around with my hat in my hand while you and this kid decide my future?"

"You decided your future. We just got sucked into helping you work it out."

Andrew was standing next to the door. He opened it for me and followed me. Neither of us said good-bye to Richard. We left him standing next to the table, looking down at the uneaten food.

"I could use a burger," Andrew said on our way out, surely the first time those words had been uttered by a diner leaving Arturo's hallowed halls.

"Me too." The wind was chilly. I thought I could smell the ocean. The neon signs on the street shone with exquisite colors.

"Let's get a couple and go to my place."

I followed him in my car and waited while he stopped at a modest-looking café called Burger Heaven, emerging with a bag that looked much too large for two hamburgers.

I understood why when, with A. J. and me watching, he began unloading its contents on his kitchen table. "They do great fries and onion rings and I couldn't decide, so I got both," he said, reaching back into the sack. "Then some guy was eating the fried mushrooms and they looked good too, so—"

"You own stock in deep fryers?"

"It's pure, all-American grease. Besides, anything we don't eat A. J. will." The last items in the bag were two cheeseburgers roughly the size of dinner plates, which were already soaking through their waxed-paper wrappers. I was almost finished with mine when I noticed Andrew smiling at me.

"What is it?"

He grinned more broadly. "It's funny. The sight of you in

your sophisticated black dress and your diamond pin, with your hair put up, sitting here with your elbows on my kitchen table eating a drippy burger and greasy fries."

"Glad to get them, too."

He swallowed his last bite and wiped his hands. "It's a turn-on. The blending of opposites, or something."

"First time I ever heard of a burger fetish."

"Another thing."

"What?"

"Your eyes. They're exactly the color of A. J.'s."

Richard, I remembered dimly, had once said apple-green jade. A. J. was under Andrew's chair, eating a French fry off a piece of waxed paper. When I bent toward him, he peered up at me. After a long look, I said, "That's a fantastic compliment."

"Listen—it's a compliment to him, too."

He came and stood behind me, nuzzling the back of my neck, his beard feeling like a loofah sponge on my skin. "I sure hope you'll stay over," he murmured. "Consider yourself invited."

"I'd love to." I nibbled on the last mushroom. "We haven't even talked about Richard's story."

"Oh yeah. Richard." I felt Andrew's warm breath on my neck when he sighed, then felt him start to pull the pins out of my hair. "I thought he handled himself pretty well up until the point when he came out with that feeble tale about the mysterious figure in the sheepskin jacket."

"That's what I thought, too. Silly of him to blow it all, right there at the end."

"My impression of Richard is that he's a damn silly man."

"Not always. He can be extremely cagey. That's what makes this so surprising."

My hair was down now. Andrew's face was buried in it. "Hey, Maggie," he said, his voice muffled.

"What?"

"Can we declare a moratorium on Richard until tomorrow morning? I've OD'd on him for right now."

131

"Let's do that." I stood and faced him. "Do you really want me to stay? I don't have a nightgown. I don't even have a toothbrush."

He put his arms around me. "You won't need a nightgown. And you can use my toothbrush. I've got a special expensive one designed by Dr. Somebody. Your gums will never be the same."

I stayed. And being with Andrew was almost enough to make me forget the horrors I had experienced and the troubles that were surely on their way.

TWENTY-FIVE

"We're agreed, then," Andrew said over coffee the next morning. "We'll go to the police as soon as you tell Candace."

I nodded. The sky was lowering, preparing for more spring rain, and the wind was high. I was through with Richard and ready to be done with him, the Golden State Center, Larry Hawkins, Joseph Corelli, and the fear and frustration they had brought me. I had to talk with Candace, and I wasn't looking forward to it, but after that it would be time to let someone else sort out the complications we had uncovered, if not unraveled.

I used Andrew's phone to call Candace. It took two accidental disconnections and a short, baffling conversation with somebody named Luis before I reached her at her dorm. When I said I wanted to drive down for a talk that afternoon, she sounded wary. "Sure, I guess it's OK, Mother, but what for?"

"I'd rather discuss it when I get there. Will three o'clock be all right?"

"I suppose so."

Irritated by her dubious tone, I said good-bye and hung up.

"My daughter thinks I'm certifiable," I said to Andrew. "Do you think your mother is certifiable?"

"No, but she does have her faults. I wish she wouldn't drive so fast."

"Tell me"—the question had been running through my mind—"how would you feel if your mother did what I'm doing? Had a—an affair, or whatever, with a much younger man?"

"Actually, once my mother made up her mind to do it, it wouldn't much matter what I felt," he said, slipping on his jacket. "She's hell for having her own way. She ran for the state senate back in Illinois last year and everybody scoffed, but she damn near won."

"But if she did have that kind of affair, would you think it was undignified and unfitting—"

"I sure would. What's more, I'd probably cut her allowance and forbid her to use the car." The phone rang and, grinning, he answered. "Baffrey. Oh, hi, Susanna. You say Maggie's not home, huh?" He gave me an exaggerated wink. "Yeah, we had a session with Richard last night. But listen"—he glanced at his watch—"I'll be seeing Maggie, and I'll tell her to be in touch with you. Maybe she can stop by your place later. Great. See you."

Turning to me, he said, "Susanna's anxious to know what went on with Richard last night. I hope you don't mind if I hand her over to you. I've got to get to the *Times* and make sure everything's moving with the Corelli issue."

"That's fine. I'll call her." I put on my coat. My black dress, so appropriate last night, looked a bit wilted this morning, but I could change when I got home. I said good-bye to Andrew on the sidewalk, promised to call him later, and headed the car toward my house.

I parked in the driveway. Preoccupied with thoughts of my talk with Candace, I didn't notice the black Lincoln across the street, or hear its door slam, so I was startled to see a stocky, curly haired man in a blue jacket approaching and hear him call my name.

He was broad shouldered, with an athletic easiness in his walk. When he got closer I saw that his eyes were the same pure light blue as his jacket. "You Maggie Longstreet?" he said.

"That's right."

"You're supposed to come with me."

I could never outrun him. He looked as if his days as a high-school fullback weren't far in the past. "Come with you where?"

"Miss Malone wants to see you."

"If Miss Malone wants to see me, she can call and set up an appointment."

"She said you should come with me." His hand closed under my elbow, and I felt myself moving toward the street.

"All right, I'll see her," I said, unnecessarily. "But couldn't I change clothes first? I need to—"

This one-sided bargaining was cut short by the slamming of the door of the Lincoln after I had been neatly placed in the back seat. My captor got into the driver's seat, started the motor, and we took off.

I gazed out the smoked-glass window, stunned. The whole episode had happened so fast it was like something I had made up to scare myself. Surely the real me was back at home letting myself in the front door, not purring toward downtown with a strong-arm chauffeur.

There was a pimple on the back of my captor's neck. "Jane Malone could have called and asked to see me," I said to it. "There was no need for this—this kidnapping."

He didn't answer, and a chill invaded my churning solar plexus. It could be he wasn't taking me to see Jane Malone at all. Maybe he had instructions to—God, to shoot me or strangle me and wrap me in a plastic garbage bag weighted with concrete blocks and dump me in the bay, and that's the end of Maggie Longstreet. Richard, all of them would claim I'd gone nuts and disappeared, wandered off or something. One of those unsolved mysteries like Judge Crater or the *Mary Celeste*.

Andrew. He wouldn't believe it. He'd raise a stink, all right. Unless, of course, he was at this very moment in the back seat of a Lincoln himself, on his way to the same fate.

My hand had crept to my throat, and my diamond pin was digging into my palm. As I eased up on it a little I thought, I'm not about to get into any garbage bags without a fight.

I needed a weapon. Mentally, I inventoried the contents of the small, dressy purse I was carrying. A lace handkerchief embroidered with a fancy *M*. Lipstick, compact, comb, keys. A wallet with about twenty dollars in it. I could offer to give him the twenty if he'd let me go. Probably not enough. I didn't have a nail file, dammit. Not even an emery board. Not that you could fight him off with an emery board, you fool.

I had a little gold portable perfume atomizer. Get in position, squirt him right in the eyes with Jolie Madame. I had—that was about all I had.

I wanted to whimper, and pressed my lips shut to avoid it. Wait a minute. I had a diamond pin. A pin that even now was making painful little indentations on the fleshy part of my palm.

With clammy fingers I fiddled with the clasp and unhooked the pin. As it came off, I felt the bar that fastened it. It was long, sturdy, and sharp. Richard had given me the pin for one of our anniversaries, and he never bought flimsy jewelry. I'd rather have had one of those cute little guns with a mother-of-pearl handle, but this would have to do. I concealed it in my hand.

My companion chose this moment to make conversation. He glanced at me in the rearview mirror, leered, and said, "Guess you were out all night, huh? I was waiting nearly an hour."

I gazed stonily out the window. We were sliding through the financial district. I watched the suicidally inclined bicycle messengers, secretaries out on errands, and stock-brokers coming in late who populated the sidewalks, wondering if any of them would pay attention if I rolled down the window and shrieked. They probably wouldn't. People who worked in downtown San Francisco were inured to weird behavior, to seeing old women yelling at random passersby, street corner preachers quizzing the indifferent crowd about being saved, down-and-outers haranguing themselves as they inspected the contents of trash cans. Yelling out of a Lincoln might type me as a rich weirdo, but only a weirdo, all the same.

At least now I was armed—or pinned. I leaned back to wait for the next development.

TWENTY-SIX

"Here we are," said the driver a minute or two later, and we turned and descended into the parking garage beneath a thirty-story glass box. I didn't think such a place would be secluded enough for mayhem at this time of day, so maybe he was taking me to Jane Malone after all. I opened my purse and put the pin inside. I'd still have easy access to it if the need arose.

He ushered me out of the car and led me to a small elevator he operated with a key. As we waited, he whistled through his teeth. Then he glanced at me sideways and said, "Have a good time last night?"

I ignored him, and he didn't make any more remarks

before we stepped out of the elevator into a room that was surely the ultimate in corporate opulence. One wall was covered with a huge woven hanging patterned in red and hot pink, and the red was repeated in oversized lacquered vases filled with eucalyptus. A leather sofa and chairs were grouped around a low, clean-lined table with a glass top. The total effect bespoke the guidance of an expensive interior designer with a blank check. After having seen Jane Malone's apartment, I was convinced that someone besides Jane had chosen the office decorator.

At a piece of furniture which resembled not a desk so much as the encircling paw of a great wooden animal sat a gray-haired woman with glasses hanging on a chain around her neck. Propelling me toward her, my companion said, "Mrs. Longstreet to see Miss Malone."

The woman beamed at me. "She's been expecting you, Mrs. Longstreet." Before I could think of a sufficiently cutting reply, she was murmuring into a telephone and then saying, "Go right in."

Jane Malone's private office was everything the anteroom had led me to expect—huge, and filled with expensive furniture and objets d'art. She was seated at a desk that contained enough wood to construct a small house. Considering her size and build, I thought something not so immense would have lessened her resemblance to a small frog on a large lily pad. Still, the overall effect was imposing.

Just inside the door the man dropped my elbow and said, "Wait here." He walked down the room and had a muttered conversation with Jane, which ended with his making a remark he apparently found amusing and she did not. Still snickering, jingling the change in his pocket, he came back to the door, gave me a last, slow look, and went out.

Jane beckoned me forward. "Come in, Mrs. Longstreet. Sit down."

"Thanks so much," I said as I marched toward her. "It

isn't as if I had a choice, is it? I'd like to know what you mean by abducting me like this."

Jane got up and walked around to the front of her desk. She was wearing an off-white suit and an apricot-colored blouse, and she looked mean as hell. "You're quite right. I didn't call up and issue an invitation. I had you brought here. There's a reason for that."

"I hope you'll tell me what it is."

"I want you to understand what you're up against, Mrs. Longstreet. I was polite the first time. You ignored me." She took a cigarette from a box on her desk and lit it. Her eyes following the smoke, she said, "I talked with Richard last night. If you got into this for revenge, you've succeeded admirably. He's frightened to death."

From the edge of contempt in her voice I could tell that no matter how thick things got for Jane Malone, being frightened to death would not be her style. "There's no reason to bully me. Try your tactics with the police. I'm out of it."

Jane's mouth twisted. "That's your fond hope. But perhaps you're in the position of the man riding the tiger in the Chinese proverb. It may be impossible to dismount."

I felt goose bumps on my arms. The woman had talent. She knew how to scare a person.

"I had you brought here to show you I was able to do it," Jane went on. "You didn't want to come and yet here you are."

"Yes. Here I am. So tell me what this show of strength is supposed to accomplish."

She disregarded the question. Studying the end of her cigarette, she said, "You spent last night with Andrew Baffrey, didn't you?"

Obviously my abductor had passed along his conjecture about my overnight absence. "That's none of your business."

"Insofar as you've interested yourself in my business,

I've become concerned with yours." She pursed her lips. "Funny. All sorts of peccadilloes are accepted these days that would've caused monumental scandals a few years back. Of course, in some sectors of San Francisco your carryings-on with young Baffrey would cause talk even today. Nothing like ostracism, perhaps, but unpleasant enough."

I laughed angrily. "If you think I'm worried that my relationship with Andrew Baffrey will get me thrown off the board of the Museum Guild, forget it."

"I wasn't thinking of that, precisely." She stubbed out her cigarette. "You and Richard have a daughter, don't you?"

Candace. All at once I saw what she was driving at. Candace, with her conventional ways, her mania for correctness, her vast respect for what people were saying. How would Candace feel when she heard gossip about her mother sleeping with the young journalist who had exposed her father as a criminal? Some daughters might be able to take it. I had a feeling that Candace couldn't. "Candace doesn't deserve to be included in this."

"Children often don't deserve the problems their parents bring on them. Richard tells me Candace is a conventional girl. She might not understand your no-doubt excellent reasons for this little fling you're having."

Jane was right. Candace wouldn't understand. She would be horrified, and she would never forgive me. Yet it was too late now to change anything, undo anything, back down. With the sense of jumping into an abyss, I decided to brazen it out. "If you think I'm worried about shocking Candace, you're mistaken. I'll save you the trouble of exposing me. I'm seeing her this afternoon, and I'll tell her myself."

Jane looked even meaner, a circumstance I would have thought impossible. "You're very lucky to have such an open relationship with your daughter." She hesitated. "Tell me. Has she been concerned about your mental state lately?"

"What do you mean?"

"Your behavior has been rather bizarre, hasn't it? Some people might believe you're having some sort of breakdown. You're depressed by your divorce, acting strangely, running around town with a man twenty years your junior, trying to embarrass your former husband. Why"—her lips stretched in a ludicrous smile—"some people wouldn't be in the least surprised if you did something drastic. Depressed, unbalanced people sometimes do, you know."

After all the fencing, we'd gotten to it at last. In a perverse way, I was almost relieved. "You mean I might kill myself. Or at least, that's how it would look."

She lifted her shoulders and let them fall.

"Is that how you did it with Larry Hawkins, too?" My voice was rising. "Got rid of him when he stood in your way?"

"Larry Hawkins had the good judgment to do it himself."

"I don't believe you! I don't—"

"I suggest you stop thinking about Larry Hawkins and begin thinking about yourself." Jane's focus on me was total. "I started as a clerk with this company. I didn't get where I am by backing down and giving in. The Golden State Center is the biggest project I've ever handled, and it *will* go through. You have to get out of my way."

I knew she was telling the truth. She had wrapped her life around a shopping mall, a high-rise office complex, and a convention center with underground parking. To threaten the Golden State Center was to threaten her, and she was fighting accordingly.

She went back to her chair and sat down. "I've said all I have to say. I hope you understand the situation."

"I do." It was quite clear. Either I stayed out of the Golden State Center business, or I would die. I felt giddy, as if I had been drinking a great deal of champagne too early in the day.

Obviously, the interview was over. I walked to the door. When I opened it to go out, I glanced back at Jane. She was still staring at me, and she stared until I closed the door on her look.

TWENTY-SEVEN

"Good-bye, Mrs. Longstreet," Jane's secretary chirped. I went past her to the glass doors leading to the corridor, assuming I wouldn't be treated to the private elevator on my way out. Stepping through the doors, I glanced around to get my bearings, and my eye caught a figure withdrawing rapidly around a corner.

Having just sustained a death threat, I was in no mood to regard rapidly withdrawing figures with equanimity. I took off in the opposite direction, searching for the elevators. I rounded a corner and saw blinking banks of them at the other end of the corridor, at the same time I heard running feet behind me. Terrified, I stumbled forward, and then a deep voice cried, "Wait!"

I knew the voice. Turning around, I nearly collided with my pursuer. It was Ken MacDonald—or the wreckage of the man.

If Ken had been on a downward spiral the other times I had seen him, he now looked as if he had hit bottom. His brushed-denim leisure suit was dust streaked, his blond hair hanging in lank clumps. His face, always flabby, had an off-center look, and he smelled like stale booze. He wouldn't have been out of place panhandling on the corner of Sixth and Mission streets. It was impossible to believe that only months ago he had been local TV's top pundit.

"Maggie," he said.

I was amazed that he had recognized me at all, much less remembered my name. Maybe it wasn't so surprising, though. I had sought him out for conversation, and that probably didn't happen to him often these days. "That's right. How are you?"

"Good, good, good." He squinted at me. "Let's go have a drink."

I had too many troubles of my own to want to listen to Ken's irrational maunderings about losing his job at Channel 8. "I'm sorry, but I really . . ."

Disappointment swept over his face. "Aw, come on," he wheedled. "I've got something to tell you."

The promise of information was no doubt a ploy, but that and the twinge of pity I felt was just enough to make me say, "I guess I have time for a quick one."

Ken's downtown drinking establishment was less hip than the Golden Raintree. We sat in a dark booth near the back of a dim, businesslike bar. When the drinks arrived, he took a long pull at his and put it down with a sigh. His face seemed to gain definition. "So," he said, looking at me expectantly.

The possibility that this meeting could be useful was becoming more remote. "You said you had something to tell me," I said. He regarded me quizzically. "About Basic Development, maybe? What were you doing there?" I prodded.

"Ha," he said, with an air that proclaimed it wasn't so easy to pull information out of Ken MacDonald. "What were *you* doing there?"

"Talking with Jane Malone."

"That bitch." Suspicion stole over his face. "You aren't working for her, are you?"

"Hardly."

He drank deeply. "Good. Because I got in trouble once, talking to a guy that worked for her."

"You mean the man who offered you the cabin at Tahoe? Nick—was it Fulton?"

"Nick Fulton. Son of a bitch offered me that cabin. Got me in trouble. Lost my job. Jane Malone's fault."

I'd heard this before, and I didn't need to hear it again. I was bored with him. "I thought it was all Larry Hawkins's fault," I said, with the unlovely motive of needling him.

"Same thing. Took me a while to figure it out, but I finally got it. Larry Hawkins, Jane Malone, same thing."

"What do you mean?"

He leaned—or, more accurately, oozed—across the table. "They were in it together. In cahoots from the beginning. Makes sense, doesn't it?"

It made no sense whatsoever. I said, "Sure." When he didn't continue, but just sat nodding wisely, I said, "In cahoots about what?"

He tapped my arm three times with his forefinger. "To get Ken MacDonald."

Only then did I realize the extent of Ken's paranoia. He had lost his job because Jane's employee, Nick Fulton, had offered him a cabin at Tahoe and Larry found out and exposed him. Therefore, Larry and Jane must be plotting against him. "Interesting theory."

"It finally came clear to me. I wrote and told Jane Malone I knew."

Jane had probably gotten a laugh out of that, if she were capable of laughing. "You told her you knew she and Larry had schemed against you?"

"I told her to watch out."

I looked at Ken closely. Was there a certain cunning, a buried cruelty, in his bleary eyes? "To watch out for what?"

He finished his drink. "Just watch out. You know what watch out means, don't you?"

"Sure, but—"

"I told her bad things happen to people who mess around with Ken MacDonald. I told her look what happened to Larry, when he messed around with Ken MacDonald. And I told her to watch out."

I sat staring. "You threatened to kill her?"

He waved his hand in front of me as if erasing my words. "Watch out. That's all I said."

"You said look what happened to Larry. What *did* happen to Larry? Do you know?"

He slumped against the back of the booth, his head lolling, all animation gone out of him. "What did happen, Ken?" I insisted.

"He went out the window. I thought you had heard about it." He closed his eyes for a few moments, then opened them and looked around vacantly. "Got to get back. Got to keep an eye on Basic."

Without further niceties he got up and shambled out of the bar. I hurried after him. When we emerged, I saw that it was beginning to rain. Ken stood swaying on the sidewalk, oblivious of the droplets spattering his clothes.

Suddenly, he gripped my arm. "There he is!" he hissed. "There he is, the son of a bitch!"

"Who?"

"Nick Fulton! The son of a bitch is across the street. See? Standing under that awning?"

I looked in the direction Ken's wavering finger pointed, and saw the man. Narrow face, thin nose, wearing a gray raincoat, smoking a cigarette. The sight of him went through me like a jolt of electricity. It was the man who had threatened me outside my garage, the man I had later seen at the Citizens Against the Golden State Center meeting. "That's Nick Fulton? The one who works for Jane Malone?"

"The son of a bitch." He shook his fist in the air. "Come here and fight, you son of a bitch!" he bellowed.

If Fulton hadn't noticed us before, he certainly did now, as did a number of passersby who noticeably speeded their gait. Fulton watched dispassionately as Ken plunged abruptly into the street, still shouting, his cries mixed with horns and squealing brakes as he dodged through the traffic. When Ken was halfway across, Fulton simply walked several yards and disappeared down an alley. Ken made it across the street and lumbered after Fulton, but I was sure there was no hope he would catch him.

I was trembling. It wasn't coincidence that Fulton had been standing across the street, and I knew he had been standing there because of me, not Ken MacDonald. Jane Malone had no intention of letting me out of reach.

It was raining harder. I had to escape while Fulton was diverted. Desperately, I scanned the street for a cab, never an easy search in San Francisco. One sailed by me, occupied. I could have wept with frustration. I half-ran down the sidewalk, rain dampening my face and hair. After a block, I looked for a cab again. Nothing. A couple of blocks ahead of me was Market Street. Buses and streetcars moved up and down it through the rain like a school of whales in a gray, turbulent sea. I could get on one, get away. I started to run.

TWENTY-EIGHT

The streetcar stop was crowded with people standing under umbrellas. Down the street, a J Church car was approaching. I was more delighted to see the dilapidated green-and-yellow vehicle grinding toward me than I would've been to receive a Rolls-Royce for my birthday. I fumbled in my purse for a quarter.

The J car pulled up. Passengers disembarked for an eternity, but finally I was able to push forward with the others waiting to get on. The seats were all taken and the aisles were jammed. I inched my way past damp bodies, shopping bags, and umbrellas to the back of the car and found a place where I could stand and hold on to the overhead bar. Clutching it, I let my knees give a little. The car doors closed, and I waited for the lurch forward that would mean I was safe. Instead of feeling the lurch, I heard pounding. As the passengers yelled "Let's go!" and "No! Go on!" the driver obligingly opened the doors. Through the crowd I saw Nick Fulton step aboard and heard the tinkle of his quarter dropping in the fare box. Then the car started to move.

I shrank back the inch I could manage. Instead of escaping, I had built myself a trap. I had never had claustrophobia before, but I experienced it now. People were jammed against me on every side, the atmosphere was stifling, and my enemy was moving closer every second.

Because Fulton was indeed getting closer. He had spotted me in one quick glance, and now was unhurriedly maneuvering toward me with an air of perfect nonchalance.

I cursed my stupidity for cornering myself in the back of the car. Now, any move I made toward the door would bring me closer to him. A young Chinese woman holding a baby was standing next to me. I leaned toward her and whispered, "Listen. I know this sounds crazy, but a man on this car is trying to get me." She avoided my eyes, shook back her long dark hair, and turned away. "You don't understand," I said. Pulling the baby closer, she maneuvered herself so her back was to me.

Fulton was standing about halfway down the car on the opposite side of the aisle. His eyes were on me, and I could no longer tear my gaze from his. My hand felt frozen to the bar, and I was hardly aware of my fellow passengers and the movement of the car.

I could never remember whether the cobra was mesmerized by the mongoose or vice versa, but anyway I couldn't stand here mesmerized like whichever one it was. I had to bolt. With a mammoth effort of will I stopped looking at Fulton. The rear door was on my side of the aisle, and I began to ease my way toward it. If I got a clear enough shot at it the next time it opened, I just might get out before Fulton could. The buzzer sounded for the next stop, and I stood poised.

I was conscious of movement from across the car, and I knew he must have realized what I was up to. All that could save me was good access to the door. I waited, muscles tensed.

The door opened quickly, but as I rushed forward an old woman with a cane, who had been standing unconcernedly at the pole next to the doorway, decided this was her stop. Unwilling to knock her flat, I shifted to the other side of the door, which was already blocked by three teenage boys with transistor radios. I got out behind them, but the delay had been too long. As I scrambled down the steps I felt Nick Fulton's hand on my upper arm and heard his low, uninflected voice saying, "I have a gun, Mrs. Longstreet. Don't make a scene."

I wanted to sit on the wet, grimy pavement and cry. If only I hadn't gotten on the streetcar. If only I hadn't—I looked at Fulton's hateful face. "What do you want?"

The bony jaw worked for a moment. "You'll find out. Let's go."

"Where?"

"Back toward downtown. We'll walk."

The rain was a steady drizzle. Moisture dripped from my hair to the inside of my coat collar. Fulton's hand never left my arm, and he stayed slightly behind me. "Why downtown?" I asked.

He didn't answer. I asked the question in a louder, more quarrelsome voice, and noticed a couple of people staring. That was good. Maybe they'd remember seeing me. "Shut up," Fulton said.

"Then answer me."

"Because my car is downtown. Now shut up."

Once he had me in a car, I would be powerless, the way I had been with Jane's driver this morning. Then I remembered. This morning I had had a plan, and I had also had a weapon. An infinitesimal flutter of hope tickled my rib cage. To disguise it, I said, "What are you going to do to me?" His answer was to tighten his grip on my arm until it hurt. "What are you going to do?" My voice was rising toward hysteria.

We were passing a flower stand, its bright offerings fragrant in the rain. "Miss Malone asked me to make sure you understood what she told you. She thinks maybe you're a hard lady to convince."

I quailed. I didn't feel at all hard to convince at that moment, but I doubted it would do any good to mention that to him. Apparently, Jane had in mind some physical roughing-up so I'd know she was serious. I swallowed several times, convulsively, at the thought.

We trudged on. Water was starting to squelch from my shoes. Ever so slowly, I slid my hand to the clasp on my purse and undid it. Thank God the pin was still near the top. I fished it up into my palm and opened it with rain-wet fingers.

I would only have an instant, and I'd have to get away fast. No more running through the streets, no more public transportation. I was trying to focus on a plan when I saw the gray stone and burgundy awnings of the St. Francis Hotel looming ahead. There was a taxi stand in front. I had gotten a cab there many times, after meeting friends for drinks in the ground-floor bar.

The awnings were closer. I could read the intertwined initials that decorated them. Several cabs were lined up in front of the canopied main entrance. I arranged the pin in my hand, holding the strong, sharp clasp bar between my fingers. A bellboy pushing a cart piled with bright red luggage emerged from the hotel, followed by a glamorous-looking young woman in a white coat. The first cab would be hers. I'd take the second.

We had reached the corner of the hotel. Across the street, the wet grass and foilage of Union Square looked impossibly green, and pigeons huddled under deserted benches. The pin was slippery. The bellboy and a cabbie were piling red bags in the first taxi's trunk. It was time. I turned as slowly as I could, gauged the distance, and sank the bar of the pin into the back of Fulton's hand.

There was a slight resistance when the point broke the skin, but after that it slid in easily. As I pulled it out he grunted, and his grip loosened. I jerked free, raced across the sidewalk to the second taxi, wrenched the door open, and jumped in. "Get me away from here," I said to the startled driver. "Now."

I had found a cabbie equal to the occasion. "Right, lady," he said, and pulled away from the curb as he put the flag down. I slid low in the seat, in case Fulton decided to use his gun, but as we increased our distance I looked back at him. He was rubbing his hand. I couldn't see the expression on his face, which was probably just as well.

The cabbie was a young man with curly hair and a shaggy mustache. He glanced over his shoulder.

"Man oh man," he said with relish, "I'll bet your date is really pissed off right now."

I slumped in the corner of the seat. "I wouldn't be surprised," I said. "I expect you're absolutely right."

TWENTY-NINE

I paid the cabbie and he drove away on a wave of good feelings and profuse thanks, the result of either the substantial tip I had given him or the drama I had contributed to his day. He had gotten me home in record time but, tempted as I was by the thought of dry shoes and fresh clothes, home wasn't where I wanted to be. With only a longing glance at the house I went to my car and got in. I wasn't about to wait until a wounded and enraged Nick Fulton arrived looking for me.

I was adrift, driving through San Francisco at random, unable to go home and with no idea what to do. Jane Malone was a respected businesswoman with friends in high places. Richard was a politico who had distributed his favors widely. That they were also crooks wasn't something the San Francisco establishment would be especially anxious to hear. It would be easy to shrug my story off as a product of hormonal imbalance or hysteria.

I might not be hormonally imbalanced, but it was obvious from the way I was driving that I *was* almost hysterical. After I made an illegal left turn that got me the finger from a post-hippie in a psychedelic van, I knew I had to stop and calm down. I was in Noe Valley. I found a parking place, walked to Twenty-fourth Street, and collapsed in a dark little coffeehouse called Grounds for Delight. Sitting at a table made from a cable spool, ingesting a bowl of vegetable barley soup and a mug of Mocha Java, I tried to get hold of myself.

The food helped. I felt rationality returning with every mouthful. By the time I had finished a piece of carrot cake and a second mug of coffee, I was ready to review my plans. The only crucial thing I had to do was drive to Stanford to see Candace, and considering the circumstances it wasn't a bad idea to get out of town. I'd start right away.

A visit to the ladies' room confirmed my worst suspicions about how I must look. For a woman who had always prided herself on being soignée, I was a major calamity. My hair had gotten very little attention since Andrew removed the pins from it the night before, and its recent soaking hadn't helped. My face was colorless, my eyes surrounded by a truly distressing network of lines. The black dress was damp and crumpled. I couldn't imagine what Candace would think—or, rather, I could. I did my best with lipstick and comb and went to pay the bill.

As I was walking out the door, I remembered my promise to Andrew that I'd be in touch with Susanna Hawkins today. Damn. On the other hand, I was ahead of time for my talk with Candace, and Susanna's place wasn't far. A short visit there would take up the slack.

Susanna's household was what any household would be with two little boys imprisoned inside on a rainy day. When I arrived, Abner and Ezekiel were pelting each other with bits of blue modeling clay, and Curly, the sheepdog, was racing around the room wearing a pink party hat with PACIFIC BAKERY ANNIVERSARY DAYS emblazoned on it. Susanna, in sweatshirt and jeans, offered me tea.

"No, thanks." I had to raise my voice to be heard over the racket. "I only stopped by for a minute to—"

She interrupted me. "Zeke, Abner, take Curly and go to your room, please. I want to talk to Maggie."

The suggestion didn't meet with a favorable response immediately, but at last some juice-and-cookie bribery was effective. Boys and dog retired semiquietly and Susanna turned to me. "Now. Did you talk to Richard?"

"Last night. He admits being at the *Times* the night Larry died, but he says he didn't kill him."

"He *does* admit being there? When?"

"He claims it must've been right after Larry went out the window. That's when he saw the folder. He panicked and grabbed it."

"Hm." Susanna seemed to be weighing what she wanted to say. "Do you believe him?"

"I don't know. He was certainly plausible enough, but under the circumstances he would be."

"What now? The police?"

"Yes."

Crayons were scattered on the floor. Susanna bent to pick them up. "I've been thinking about it. You know, Larry was threatened constantly. I guess it isn't so surprising that somebody decided to kill him. Now that I've gotten used to the idea, it seems reasonable."

"Apparently Richard was one of those who threatened. Oh—another thing. After we told him about our suspicions, Richard came up with a story about seeing somebody leave the *Times* that night."

Her hand hovered over a yellow crayon. "He did? Who did he see?"

"He said he didn't recognize the person. It was a figure in a sheepskin jacket with a hood, someone who came out of the building and hurried away. But as I say, he only remembered under duress. It struck Andrew and me that it was probably a last-minute fabrication."

She stood. "That's what it sounds like. Something he made up to take attention away from himself."

Just then the boys tumbled into the room screaming, "Juice, Mommy! We want more juice!" and I moved to leave.

As Susanna handed me my coat, she said, "Are you convinced that Richard killed Larry?"

The question made me uncomfortable. "Convinced" was an extremely final word. "I think there's a chance that he did. I'm not totally convinced." I wondered why I hadn't said that to Andrew.

"I see," said Susanna thoughtfully, and we said good-bye.

Although the rain had lessened to intermittent spatters, the freeway traffic was terrible and the hour's drive south down the Peninsula to Palo Alto grueling. Off the freeway at last, I drove toward Stanford through sedate, tree-lined streets and wondered if I was going to see Candace for the last time. Children did reject their parents, break with them forever. It had happened to friends of mine in the sixties. I had never imagined I would have to worry about dutiful Candace doing it to me.

The Spanish-style red-tile roofs of the campus buildings

glistened wetly under the brightening sky, and with its lush vegetation and students loitering on steps or whizzing by on bicycles Stanford seemed a haven of tranquility. I found Candace's dorm. Standing outside the door of her room, I hesitated. Coming down here to talk with her had been my idea. I could walk away, phone from a filling station in Palo Alto, say I wasn't coming, let matters take their course without this confrontation. Instead, I knocked on the door and heard her calling to me to come in.

When I entered, she got up from her desk and said, awkwardly, "Hi, Mother."

"Hi." She was wearing white denim jeans and a sea-green sweater. The color made her look blonder and more delicate, her face unnaturally pale. She was looking at me, I thought, with something like dread. I was sure she had spoken to Richard.

"Sit down." She gestured to one of the twin beds with bright striped covers that were placed against opposite walls. I sat on the edge of the bed, and she resumed her seat at the desk. For a few moments, we watched each other.

Completely at a loss, I lapsed into inanity. "You're looking worn out. Have you been studying too hard?"

She made a gesture of impatience. "Mother, I talked to Daddy this morning."

"What did he say?"

She took a deep breath. "He told me you've gotten very strange ideas about him. He said you've misinterpreted some of his business dealings, and you're going to get him in a lot of trouble."

It wasn't that Richard ever made mistakes—only that other, inferior beings didn't understand him. But could I blame him, really, for wanting to maintain his image with Candace? "I don't think I misinterpreted anything," I said carefully. "I saw the proof. Your father took a bribe. He didn't even deny it when I confronted him."

"He told me that, too. He"—she started to sniffle—"he

said he knew it looked bad, but it was business and what he did wasn't anything unusual."

"That's probably true. Do you think it's all right, since it's common practice?"

"Oh, Mother—" she began to cry in earnest. "Please don't expose him. I know he won't do it again. He promised he wouldn't. *Please*." Shaking with sobs, she buried her face in her hands.

It was worse than I had imagined. I had assumed Candace would be stiff and accusing. I never thought she'd plead with me. And here was the insidious part. If I did what she wanted this time, maybe she'd feel differently about me from now on. I crossed the room and stroked the bent blonde head. How old had she been the last time I had done this? Ten? Twelve?

"The bribe isn't even the worst," I said. "You know, Larry Hawkins died, and another man has died since. I'm afraid your father may be mixed up in that too, somehow."

She shuddered and shook my hand away. "That's just *crazy*!" she protested, sounding strangled with tears.

"It isn't crazy. Don't say that to me."

She looked up, her face blotched with red. "Why shouldn't I say it? How do you think you've been acting? This whole thing is totally insane!"

I turned my back on her and walked to the window. It looked out on a magnolia tree with large, slippery-looking, dark-green leaves. I let the echoes of her voice die, in the room and in my head, before I spoke. "I'm having an affair with a—a much younger man. His name is Andrew Baffrey, and he's the editor of the *People's Times*. I'm telling you because you may hear it elsewhere."

"Great." The syllable was filled with distress, but not surprise. Richard had probably preceded me with that news, too.

"I wanted you to know."

"Thanks a *lot*." Candace's voice was scathing. "On top of everything else that's fabulous, Mother! What am I

154

supposed to do, congratulate you on how far you'll go to get even with Daddy? What's next? Are you going to go with this guy to his senior prom?"

"Shut up." I hadn't known I was going to shout. "I'm trying to treat you like an adult, and you're acting like a damned teenage idiot. I will not be tyrannized by you, Candace, or by your father, or by anyone else. Perhaps you don't realize it, but I love you, and . . ." All of a sudden, I had run out of things to say. I sat back down on the bed, biting my lip, not looking at her.

She didn't make a sound. Her crying had stopped, and I didn't even know if she was breathing. After a minute or two, almost inaudibly, she said, "OK, Mother."

My throat was tight. "What do you mean?"

"I'm not sure. Just OK."

"Candace, I've been so frightened . . ." I knew I'd better not go on. She looked shaken, and desperately unhappy. Confidences would have to wait.

"You know I don't want you to do this to Daddy," she said.

"And you know I believe I have to."

She nodded bleakly. I walked to the door, and she followed me. I turned to her and rested the palm of my hand against her face. "The next few days are going to be difficult," I said.

Her eyes filled with tears. I held her for a moment, and felt the brief pressure of her arms around me. Then I kissed her on the cheek and walked out the door.

Something momentous had happened. My chest felt swollen, about to burst. Unwilling to drive away yet, I walked a few blocks under the dripping trees. At least she hadn't told me she would never forgive me. At least she had put her arms around me when we said good-bye. I returned to the car for the long drive back to San Francisco.

THIRTY

The return-trip traffic was ferocious, and the afternoon was waning by the time I reached the *Times*. I hoped the Corelli issue was on the streets and Andrew was ready to play the last act in our too exciting drama. I heard phones ringing before I walked into the office, and the first thing I saw was a frazzled-looking Betsy O'Shea, her red hair wilder than ever. She had the phone receiver tucked between her ear and shoulder while both hands searched through one of her desk drawers. Several of the buttons on her phone were blinking, indicating other callers on hold.

"Sorry, I can't seem to locate it right now," she was saying. "Sure, I'll call as soon as I do. Bye." Putting down the receiver, she said, "What a time to call about a restaurant review, for God's sake."

"Looks like you're busy."

She indicated the blinking lights. "It's been this way all day. The Corelli story really lit up the skies. The wire services picked it up, and it may be on Walter Cronkite, too."

"Great for the paper."

"Fantastic. We may break even this issue." She punched a button and said, *"Times."*

A celebratory atmosphere prevailed in the newsroom. Two gallon jugs of wine, one red and one white, sat on a desk, along with part of a loaf of sourdough and some hacked-looking cheese. Members of the staff were standing around drinking wine out of coffee mugs and talking animatedly. In one group, a young woman read aloud from one of the daily papers while her companions laughed uproariously at every sentence. "They *completely* botched it," she crowed as she finished the story.

The one element missing from the happy scene was the triumphant editor himself. Andrew was nowhere in sight. I found his office empty, and after waiting awkwardly to one side for a few minutes in case he'd gone to the bathroom I returned to Betsy in the outer office.

When I asked, she pounded her forehead with her fist. "How dumb can I be? It's these damn phones. I completely forgot to tell you he went to your place."

A sick feeling unfolded in my stomach. "My place? Why? How long ago?"

She screwed her eyes closed. "Let's see—twenty minutes ago, maybe? He said something about not being able to get you on the phone and making a swing by there to check things out. I thought maybe he wanted to bring you back to the party." Her eyes popped open. "Sorry I forgot."

I was already out the door and halfway to the elevator before she could say, "Hey, Maggie! Is everything all right?" and as I leaned on the button I felt dizzy. Andrew would have no idea that Nick Fulton was likely to be watching my place, and even if I were Fulton's preferred victim, Andrew would probably do in a pinch. I cursed impetuous youth, which led to actions like prancing off to check things out when you couldn't get people on the phone. He'd known I was going to Stanford, hadn't he? But the traffic had been bad and the trip had taken longer than it normally would. Besides which, dammit, he'd been worried about me. Now I was plenty worried about him.

The drive to my place was a nightmare of clogged streets, exhaust fumes, and ever-more-vivid mental images of the various horrible fates that might have befallen Andrew. When I finally reached Lake Street it seemed, after the cataclysms of my imagination, surreally quiet and empty. There, indeed, was Andrew's Volkswagen with its rear-bumper plea to boycott Gallo, parked a block from my house. There was my house itself, the picture of serenity in the twilight. I didn't see Nick Fulton, the stocky man who'd driven the Lincoln, or anyone at all who looked like a possible member of Jane Malone's goon squad.

Strangely, perhaps the appearance of normality agitated me all the more. I was blinking back tears by the time I parked in the driveway. Andrew couldn't be in the house, since he had no key. He wasn't in the front yard. In a frenzy of anxiety, I ran toward the back.

It was dark enough by now for the park to be deserted. Tennis players, joggers, old men with their checkerboards, babies in strollers had all gone home to dinner. The blossoms of the almond tree outside my glassed-in back room were almost luminous in the deepening dusk. A petal floated down, lightly brushing my cheek as I tried to call Andrew's name, didn't manage it, cleared my throat and tried once more.

No answer came, and I plunged across the narrow footpath and into the park proper. Wet grass brushed my ankles. I ran a few yards and called again.

The first shot didn't faze me. If I had time to think at all, I may have thought it was a car backfiring. It was the second, which knocked bark off a Douglas fir not far at all from where I stood, that enlightened me about what was happening. Instinctively, I turned to run. As the third shot sounded, I tripped over a root and fell full-length in the grass.

I was dazed, winded, and not at all sure I wasn't wounded as well. All I knew was that if Jane Malone herself were charging me with a red-hot revolver I couldn't move, much less get up and run. I struggled for breath, blades of grass tickling my nostrils and ears, and in a few moments I heard running feet and Andrew's voice calling, "Maggie!"

He was bending over me, gibbering something about oh my God, where are you shot, and I managed to gasp, "Not shot."

He blotted his eyes on his sleeve and said, "It came from over there. I'll go see," and I didn't have the wind to tell him not to be an idiot. Expecting every minute to hear more shots followed by his dying groans, I struggled up to one elbow. In fact, I heard nothing and shortly he returned to kneel beside me again.

"Nobody there, but I found this beside a bush," he said.

The object in his palm looked, in the fading light, like a piece of wadded cloth or paper. I touched it. "What is it?"

"A glove, I think. Let's go in."

I could stand now, and he helped me totter to the door. The house had an air of neglect, as if it had stood empty for much longer than twenty-four hours. I lay on the sofa, and he turned on an end-table lamp and placed his find in the pool of light.

It was a glove, crumpled into a ball, as if it had been wadded and carelessly thrust into the bottom of a pocket. Too bad, because good pigskin driving gloves were expensive. Richard had a pair like that. Candace gave them to him Christmas before last, right after he got the Porsche. Pigskin driving gloves, holes over the knuckles, and inside on the hem the initials *RL* stamped in gold. Yes. There were the initials.

"That's odd," I said.

"What's odd?" Andrew sounded hoarse.

"This glove looks like Richard's. It even has his initials in it. See?"

"Maybe that's because it's Richard's glove," he said quietly.

"It couldn't be. Richard adored his gloves. He took exquisite care of them. Candace gave them to him. He would never . . ." I realized how ridiculous I must sound.

"Maggie, Richard tried to kill you." Andrew's face had a peculiar, zealous intensity.

"It wasn't Richard. It was Nick Fulton." I gave him a

quick rundown of my adventures with Fulton and Jane Malone.

When I finished, he said, "Still. Why would Nick Fulton have Richard's glove? Richard shot at you. Face it."

Was I simply being perverse. "It's completely unlike him to wad up his glove like that."

After a moment or two, Andrew stood up. "I'll bet you could use a drink."

"Not to mention a bath." He poured brandy and handed it to me, and I said, "What were you doing? Where were you when I got here?"

He poured himself a drink and sat down. "We had incredible excitement over the Corelli story, you know? But all day long, Maggie, I swear there wasn't a minute I wasn't worried about you. I thought, there's danger everywhere, and you were out there in it, and I kept wishing I'd had you come to the *Times* with me so I could keep tabs on you. I knew you'd gone to Stanford, but I kept calling here and there was no answer and I thought you should've been back. I kept thinking maybe you had gotten back and Richard had come over and done something to you, which"—he shot me a glance—"is exactly what I believe did happen.

"Toward late afternoon I couldn't stand it any longer, so I hopped in the car and came out here. Of course you weren't here, but as long as I'd made the trip I got some wild-assed notion of checking things out, seeing if anybody was making suspicious moves. That's what I was doing when I heard the shots. Somebody *was* making suspicious moves, but in a different part of the park."

"I guess we're lucky neither of us got killed."

"We sure are." He put his drink down and stood. "OK, Maggie. Now let's take the damn glove, go to the police, and tell them about Richard."

THIRTY-ONE

It wasn't easy, but I convinced Andrew that I had to have a bath before we went to the police. He followed me to the bedroom and leaned in the doorway while I wearily peeled off the black dress. I'd give it to Goodwill. I never wanted to wear it again.

"I almost forgot to tell you. The scuttlebutt is that there's a lead in the Corelli case," he said.

"Really?"

"Yeah. Three old guys were sitting at Luigi's drinking Chianti when the murder happened. One of them thinks he saw a man getting in a car at the end of the alley and driving away about that time. The only problem is, the other two don't remember anything, and this old fellow has cataracts or something, so they're not sure how good his information is."

"What kind of car?"

"He doesn't remember a make—just that it was big and blue."

Richard didn't have access to any blue cars that I knew of. His agency car was black, and the Porsche was dark green. Anyway, why the hell was I thinking up excuses for Richard? I pulled on my salmon-colored peignoir. "I'm going to soak. Be with you in a little while."

When I sank into the tub, surrounded by cucumber-scented bubbles from Candace's organic bath oil, I closed my eyes and tried to turn off my mind. The hot water felt as if it were dissolving me all the way down to my bones.

In a few minutes, I was struggling across an alien landscape—crawling over dun-colored hills, clambering into creased valleys, then pulling myself up hills again. It was so difficult I almost cried with frustration. As far as I could see, there were more brown hills. Then I realized that the ground I was standing on wasn't really earth. It had a bumpy, elastic texture—I woke with a start. The landscape I had been crawling over was Richard's crumpled pigskin glove.

The water was tepid. I shivered and got out, dried myself briskly, and put on boots, blue wool pants, a white turtleneck. Andrew was standing in the living room. "Ready to go?" he said when I walked in.

I had no choice. "I have something to tell you."

He smiled. "Speak."

"I don't believe Richard shot at me tonight. I think someone is trying to make things look bad for him. I can't go to the police and accuse him of something I don't believe he did."

Andrew's face stiffened. "Why don't you think he did it? What about the glove?"

"The glove is the reason. Richard was very fond of those gloves, and he wouldn't treat them like that. It's against his nature."

"What about Larry? Do you think he killed Larry?"

I shook my head. "I don't believe he shot at me tonight, and I don't believe he killed Larry, either. Somebody's trying to frame him."

Andrew looked grim, remote. "I saw this coming. Saw it a mile off. Ever since we started this thing, you've shied away from believing Richard was guilty. You'd rush forward one step and fall back two. Do you admit it?"

"No, I don't. I was always perfectly willing—"

"Why don't you face facts? You were angry with Richard for leaving you and you wanted to make him sweat, and that's all there was to it. You were never serious about the investigation."

I had been threatened, shot at, abducted. I had discovered a dead body. I wasn't serious about the investigation? "I've never been so serious about anything!"

"Yet you won't go to the police when you know Richard's guilty."

"I *don't* know he's guilty! I won't go because I don't believe he killed anybody. The bribery, yes. Fine. But I don't think Richard or anybody else should be wrongfully accused of murder."

"So what do you propose to do now?" His demeanor was elaborately polite.

"I'm going to ask Richard about his gloves and see what his explanation is, and—"

"Then you'll have to do it by yourself!" Andrew exploded. "I've had enough kowtowing to Richard and asking his explanation for everything!"

I retreated into frigidity. "If that's the way you want it, fine. There's no reason to continue discussing it."

He thrust his hands angrily into his jacket pockets and started for the door. He stopped once and threw me a bitter glance, then the door slammed and he was gone.

I stood motionless in the living room, stunned by the intensity of our fight—how quickly it had sprung up, how hotly it had raged. I was also overcome by déjà vu. Not so long ago, Richard had stormed out. Now Andrew had done the same thing. I wondered if life consisted of playing the same scenes over and over, with different actors.

I was stung by Andrew's defection. Even considering the strain we'd been under, his response struck me as an overreaction. He had been my friend, my confidant, my lover, my co-investigator. Now he was so anxious to nail Richard that it all meant nothing. An unpleasant thought entered my head. Was he perhaps too anxious to nail Richard? I had only his word for where he was when the shooting was going on, only his word that he had found Richard's glove in the park. He could've had it in his pocket the whole time.

Andrew could have been working to frame Richard, to convince me that Richard killed Larry. Why? Maybe Andrew killed Larry himself. Andrew was in charge of the *Times* now. He and Larry hadn't always gotten along. Maybe something boiled over that night, and . . .

I felt dirty. How could I possibly suspect Andrew? Surely he had done a thousand things that proved his innocence. But had he, really?

I didn't want to think about it anymore. I had something else to do. An advantage of my fall in the grass was that whoever had shot at me probably thought I was dead or wounded. Nobody would be watching the house. I could come and go as I pleased.

I picked up the glove, put it in my purse, and went out. I got in the car and headed for Russian Hill to see Richard.

THIRTY-TWO

Although his job required him to be an apostle of the new, Richard had always preferred the old when choosing his own residences. He was living in the Towers, an ever-so-elegant Russian Hill apartment building dating from the twenties which was elaborately decorated with terra-cotta mermaids, dolphins, seashells, and varied picturesque flotsam. A uniformed man in the unobtrusively sumptuous lobby announced me on the telephone and told me to go up to apartment 3-A.

In the silent, mirrored elevator with its polished brass fittings I wondered if I'd been wrong, if I were putting myself in danger by coming here. I almost wished I could change my mind, believe Richard was trying to kill me. If I believed that, Andrew and I could be together again. I tried, but I couldn't.

Voices came from apartment 3-A, and before I rang the bell I stood listening. Richard's part of the conversation was an indistinct monotone, but an agitated female exclamation, "Well, I won't! I'm staying!" was clearly audible.

My God. Was it possible that I had completely forgotten about the woman whose reputed charms I had brooded on for hours, whose existence had led me to constant tranquilizers and musings about suicide? I had come here without stopping to consider that the visit would probably bring me face to face with Diane, the law student Richard had left me for. A confrontation I had played in my mind thousands of times, always with myself in a wounded but dignified role, was about to take place. Not only was I unprepared for it, I wasn't even interested in playing it through.

When Richard opened the door I noticed the familiar lines of irritation around his eyes and mouth. But when I entered the room I realized that this time, for a change, the lines hadn't been caused by vexation with me. The young woman standing by the fireplace with her hands on her hips, half-glaring at Richard, looked as exasperated as he did.

"Maggie, this is Diane. Diane, Maggie," said Richard. Under the circumstances he did it smoothly, I thought. Leaving off the last names was a good touch.

"How do you do." I could hear traces of temper in Diane's voice. Richard's attempt to exclude her from the conversation had apparently struck a nerve. I looked at her curiously. She was a slim, tanned, attractive woman in her twenties with very short taffy-blonde hair by Clairol, a freckle-sprinkled nose, and blue eyes. Tennis court looks. A certain determination about her mouth told me that when she played she liked to win. She wore gold hoop earrings, a yellow turtleneck, and gray tweed slacks—an outfit very much like the one I was wearing. She was a nice-looking girl, I thought with detachment, but she really had nothing to do with me.

After returning her greeting, I turned to Richard and said, "I'm sorry for barging in, but I came to ask whether you still have the driving gloves Candace gave you Christmas before last."

He looked very surprised. "Why the hell would you ask that?"

"Do you have them?"

His mouth contorted. "As a matter of fact, I don't. They were stolen out of the car yesterday afternoon. Just another rotten episode among many that have happened lately. Why?"

I took the glove, still crumpled, out of my purse and showed it to him. He looked at it blankly, then back at me. "That was a good glove, for God's sake," he said. "Couldn't you have managed not to wad it up?" His eyes narrowed. "Where'd you get it, anyway?"

"It was dropped by somebody who shot at me tonight."

"Who did *what*?" Richard looked genuinely shocked as I launched into the story. Diane stood unmoving by the fireplace.

When I finished, Richard shook his head. "You say this happened around six? Well, I was here then. I was already here. Wasn't I, Diane?"

"Yes, you were." Her voice was firm, but I believed she would lie for him. I wondered how much she knew about Richard's current problems, and whether she'd latched on to more than she'd bargained for when she got him.

Apparently worried by my silence, Richard rushed in again. "Like I told you, they were stolen yesterday. I had stopped at the little wine importer in the Pacific Bakery Mall to pick up a few bottles of the Bordeaux Diane likes." Did the look he shot Diane contain an element of blame? "Anyway, I was rushing because I had to meet you and Baffrey, and I had a great deal on my mind, and I must've forgotten to lock the car. I'm lucky the whole damn Porsche wasn't stolen. Anyway, I thought I'd be just a minute, but they were having some kind of promotion and I had to fight my way through it. When I got back to the car, the gloves were gone." He was defiant. "That's what happened."

"I believe you," I said.

Richard's face sagged in disbelief. "You do?"

"Yes. I think someone's trying to make it look as if you murdered Larry Hawkins."

"Oh God, Maggie, I . . ." Richard sat down on the couch, his eyes red. Diane moved swiftly and sat beside him, putting her arm around his shoulders. The scene embarrassed me, mostly because I thought Diane was playing it for my benefit. Richard was now hers to comfort, to protect, she was telling me. She was welcome to him.

I looked away, studying the living room. What struck me was its similarity to my own. The carpets were rough-woven Peruvian instead of Oriental, and there were pre-Columbian figurines instead of Daumier etchings, but the essential feeling of careful good taste was the same. Richard had placed his imprint on his new home as surely as he had on his former one. I wondered if he would do that with his new woman, too—as thoroughly as he had with me.

After a minute or two Richard spoke, hoarsely. "Who would try to frame me?"

"I don't know. I thought you'd have some suggestions."

"No. I can't think." He was silent. Then, his voice shot through with hope, he said, "Does this mean you won't tell the police?"

"I won't say anything about Larry's death in relation to you. You'll still have to answer for the bribery. You're on your own there."

"I see." Richard looked worn out, enfeebled, like a very old man. In contrast, Diane was smooth, uncreased, self-possessed. For a moment, it seemed that Richard had invested all his former attributes in her. Then he regained his presence and said, almost normally, "Let's have a drink. How about Scotch? Still a Scotch drinker?"

"Scotch would be fine."

"I'll get some ice." He left the room, and Diane and I were alone. She looked at me directly, keenly. "This has been terribly upsetting for Richard," she said.

I was nettled. I didn't want to discuss Richard as if I were his mother and she his first-grade teacher. "Richard ought to be delighted he's not going to face questioning for murder."

"Yes, of course. But this bribery thing. It's going to be hard on him."

"I expect it is."

She glanced over her shoulder, making sure he wasn't coming back. "You don't think—it wouldn't be possible to—" She stopped, studying her gray tweed knees. "Couldn't you just forget about it?" The words came out rapidly, and her scarlet face told me how difficult they had been to say.

"I couldn't." Whether she had been trying to or not, she had made me feel sorry for her. "It isn't up to me alone, anyway, but even if it were I'd have to say no."

"Oh." Her voice trailed off in a long sigh.

Richard came back, holding an ice bucket. "Sorry I took so long. Diane, the refrigerator is acting up again. The ice is hardly frozen."

I was sorry I'd agreed to a drink. Diane and Richard were making me feel claustrophobic. Whatever was happening between them, I wanted it to happen without me. I'd finish fast and get out. As I sipped my drink, I remembered Andrew's news about the Corelli murder. I had never really understood what Richard's relationship with Corelli had been. "I hear they have a lead in the Corelli killing," I said.

"Oh?" Richard sounded only minimally interested.

"Yes." I decided to ask. "What exactly did Corelli have to do with the Golden State Center, anyway?"

Richard gulped his drink. "Corelli was the worst of the obstructionist bastards. He owned a corner of the site, and by God he was going to hang on to it. I argued with him till hell wouldn't have it. Jane talked to him several times, and he still held out. Thought we could do better moneywise, so he had a whole battery of delaying tactics he was threatening us with. May Corelli rest in peace, and all that, but his getting killed didn't hurt us a bit. His number-two man took over, and he's being a lot more cooperative."

Strange. Richard talked as if his entire house of cards wasn't going to fall on him. He obviously couldn't accept the fact that he was going to face a bribery scandal. The thought made me even more anxious to leave. I finished my drink, said good-bye, and turned to go. Diane walked me to the door. I saw the strain in her pretty face. She knew what was in store, even if Richard wouldn't admit it. "I hate to beg," she whispered, "but I will if you make me."

I could only shake my head. I stepped across the threshold and the door closed behind me. I was out, and free.

THIRTY-THREE

There was a window in an alcove at the end of the hall. Light-headed, I walked to it, trying to regain my mental and physical balance in the wake of emotional overload, a too strong drink, and no dinner. I looked out on light-spangled San Francisco. Burned down over and over, shaken by earthquakes hundreds of times and all but destroyed in 1906, it had grown again, prospered again, become new like the phoenix on the city and county seal. I rested my forehead on the glass. I shouldn't have had that drink. I was getting sentimental about a town where political corruption was as common as low-lying fog. I was allowing myself to wonder whether my life, too, like San Francisco's phoenix—

I was saved from sloppiness by hearing the elevator door open. Curious to see who was visiting Richard, I looked around the corner and saw two men walking toward his door. One of them I had never seen before. The other was Inspector Fred Bosworth of the San Francisco Police Department. I watched him ring Richard's bell. When the door opened, he said, "We're looking for Richard Longstreet," and the two men stepped inside.

I leaned against the windowsill, wondering what Bosworth wanted with Richard. Bosworth had been working on the Corelli case. Maybe he wanted to question Richard about Corelli. That must be it.

Yet why would Bosworth show up to question Richard about Corelli tonight? He had had time to see Richard at his office, or to call and make an appointment to stop by. I was sure Richard hadn't been expecting the police when he talked to me. I longed to listen at the door, but decided against it.

The explanation came to me while I rode down in the elevator. Bosworth wasn't talking to Richard about Corelli, he was talking about Larry. And why? Because Andrew had gone to the police himself. Andrew was, after all, over twenty-one, if just barely. He didn't have to hold off because I said so. He had gone, he had accused Richard, and here was Inspector Bosworth. Ironically, about the time I was assuring Richard he wouldn't be questioned about Larry's death, Andrew was arranging that he would. Richard probably thought I had betrayed him, but there was nothing I could do about it now.

I walked to the car and started home. This was no time to be choosy about dinner, so I turned in at the first fast-food outlet I saw, which happened to be purveying fried chicken to go.

The interior of the place was bathed in a pale neon glare that made the strawberry pies in the glass cabinet look as much like plastic as they probably tasted. The ambience wasn't helped by a radio blaring rock music. There were three people ahead of me—two young men in tight jeans and T-shirts who were whispering to each other and laughing, and a woman with limp gray hair who was carrying a shopping bag containing, as far as I could tell, some articles of clothing and a picture of Jesus.

The two men were having trouble deciding whether to get a regular or a jumbo bucket. I leaned against the counter and closed my eyes, numbed by the noise and glare. The frenetic radio announcer was bawling something about "news time." No more music for a minute or two, anyway. The woman in front of me ordered a whole strawberry pie and a Coke. The thought made the inside of my mouth feel puffy.

"What would you like, ma'am?" a stringy-haired girl in a paper hat asked me.

"I'll have—"

"—Corelli, local restaurant owner," said the radio.

"What?" The girl leaned forward.

I shook my head and made violent shushing motions with my hand.

"—spokesman said that Fresno police are holding Nick Fulton, who has former convictions on robbery and assault charges, for murder. Fulton was apprehended in a Fresno motel late this afternoon. On the weather scene—"

The girl leaned her elbows on the counter, making designs on the Formica with her finger. Obviously, she was prepared to wait through the weather and sports if necessary. My pulses were pounding. Nick Fulton was in custody. The blissful relief I felt made me realize how frightened I had been of him.

On the other hand, if he had been in Fresno this afternoon, he couldn't possibly be the person who'd shot at me.

At home in my kitchen, gnawing through globs of greasy fried batter, I tried to collect my thoughts and assess what was going on.

Since Nick Fulton had been arrested, probably the old man Andrew mentioned had been able to identify him. Fulton was the man in the blue car. Richard had said Corelli was causing problems for the Golden State Center. In Jane Malone's lexicon, that was reason enough for violence—especially if Corelli's number-two man were amenable to Basic Development's plans. They had tried everything else—persuasion from Richard and Jane, and coercion. Suddenly I remembered the break-in at the *Times*. Richard had known that Larry was blackmailing Corelli. He had probably told Jane about it. If they could locate Larry's information, they could have used it against Corelli themselves. The break-in had been an unsuccessful attempt to find the information Susanna had gotten from Larry's safe-deposit box.

Maybe Fulton knew I had discovered Corelli's body, and that had given him extra motivation for wanting me out of the way. At first, though, he must have thought he wasn't in danger. He'd stayed in town until the situation started to heat up. When he finally ran, he made it only as far as Fresno.

I crumpled my cardboard box with its chicken bones and its little Styrofoam cup of runny coleslaw and threw it in the garbage can. I was sure Fulton had killed Corelli on Jane Malone's orders, or at least with her tacit agreement. Of course it would come out that Fulton worked for her. Jane Malone's dream was over, Richard's career was in ruins, Nick Fulton was in jail, Corelli was dead, and Larry—what about Larry?

I wandered into the living room. The little snifter that had held Andrew's brandy sat on the coffee table. I carried it into the kitchen. I could go back to square one. Maybe Larry committed suicide after all. No. That wouldn't work.

Somebody had shot at me, and that meant somebody was afraid. Suicide wasn't a reasonable explanation.

My head was buzzing. I went back into the living room and sat on the couch. I had to face the suspicions of Andrew that, below the surface, had been tearing at me all evening. Once I decided to explore my misgivings about him, though, the case became elusive. He could've killed Larry and shot at me, I thought, but my mind kept returning to Andrew making me a salami sandwich, or pulling the pins out of my hair, or being with me in bed.

He can't be innocent just because you want him to be, I reprimanded myself. Did you ever ask him where he was the night of the murder? Of course not. Richard says he saw a figure in a sheepskin jacket leaving the *Times*. You spent an entire night at Andrew's place. Did it ever occur to you to check in his closet to see if he has a sheepskin jacket? No. You had other things on your mind.

Maybe another drink would help. Another drink, and then bed. Tomorrow everything would be clear, rationality would return, I would put my life in order and lead a clean, healthy, sensible existence to a ripe old age if I didn't get shot first.

I went to the liquor cabinet and took out the Scotch. As I set it down and reached for a glass, I knew who Larry's murderer was.

The knowledge immobilized me for some seconds. As I stood with my hand outstretched, I ran through it all in my mind. The facts backed up my intuitive flash. Larry Hawkins had been murdered, and I knew who had done it. I let my arm drop. It would probably be best if I didn't have another drink tonight.

THIRTY-FOUR

I couldn't prove it, but I'd be able to soon. I sat at my desk and began to write.

The whole story came to only a page and a half. I folded the scrawled sheets, put them in an envelope, wrote the address. I'd mail it on the way.

Driving through the city, stopping to drop the envelope in a mailbox, I felt, at last, relaxed and competent. It had been only a few days—less than a week—since Larry Hawkins died, but I knew I would never be the same. I could no more return to pills and lamentations now than I could reactivate my membership in the Museum Guild and be a society divorcée instead of a society matron. Which posed a problem. I would have to work out something to do.

Musings about the future would have to wait, however. I had reached my destination. I parked, crossed the street, and pushed the bell.

No answer. I rang again. I could see a dim light inside. Stumbling through weeds, I made my way around the side of the house. After scraping my shin climbing over a rickety fence, I was in the backyard. The light I had seen was coming from the kitchen. There was a gap in the kitchen window curtains, and I looked through it and saw Susanna Hawkins shrinking into a corner next to the stove, arms crossed and hands clutching her elbows, her head cocked in a listening attitude.

I called, "Susanna!" and tapped on the window.

She started violently. Her eyes darted to a drawer next to

her, and she pulled it open and reached inside. Then she closed it again and buried her face in her empty hands.

"Susanna! It's Maggie!" Even standing as far away as I was, I saw the shudder that ran through her body. Then she became instantly mobilized, as if I had thrown a switch. She dashed to the window, threw the curtains back, and stared out at me. The bones of her face seemed to stretch her delicate skin, and her eyes were wide. Only her hair retained the appearance of health. It mantled her shoulders, reflecting light from the room behind her.

When she saw me she sank to her knees, resting her forehead on the windowsill. "Let me in!" I called. She got up, looking dazed, and moved toward the back door. When she opened it, I said, "You see, you didn't kill me after all."

"I wasn't trying to," she whispered.

She stepped back and I walked past her. In a corner Curly eyed me sleepily, his tail thumping the floor. We walked to the living room, where a red wooden child-sized chair was lying on its side. Susanna righted it and sat down in it, knees together and feet spread apart. "I wasn't trying to kill you," she said. "I nearly fainted when I saw you fall down."

"Why were you shooting, then?"

"Oh, you know," she said almost absentmindedly, as if it no longer mattered. "I wanted to make sure you went to the police about Richard. I was afraid you were wavering."

"You stole Richard's gloves?"

"I had to. Once you decided somebody killed Larry, I wanted you to be positive it was Richard. You were on the brink. I left the boys with the neighbors. . . ." She giggled. "Isn't that funny? To have to worry about getting a baby-sitter so you can go out and steal and shoot at people?" She giggled louder, and I was afraid she would become hysterical, but she stopped with a choked gasp.

"How did you get the gloves?"

"Easy." Her face started to collapse again, but she

mastered it. "I made up a story about an insurance policy and called Richard's office and found out what kind of car he drives. I hung around his building until he left and followed him. I wasn't sure what I was going to do. I thought I'd follow him to his place, and maybe there'd be a chance to break in, get something of his—I don't know. I was wild." She shook her hair back from her face. "His leaving the car unlocked at Pacific Bakery was sheer luck for me. I grabbed the gloves."

"Tonight you came and waited at my house."

"When I got there you weren't home. I stood in the park. I thought I'd shoot and break a window or something, but you had to be there or it wouldn't work. I had Richard's glove in my pocket, and I had Larry's gun. He kept one here, because he was afraid his enemies would come gunning for him in the middle of the night. I had no idea you'd run into the park. God, you were coming right at me. I shot, but I wasn't trying to kill you. Not the way I was trying to kill Larry."

"He was going to leave you."

"That's what the note was about. He was going to run out without saying a word, the lousy coward."

I remembered the cryptic "Sorry to do this to you and the kids." Not much in the way of a parting message. That afternoon, Andrew had confronted Larry and told him he knew Larry was blackmailing Corelli. Larry must have believed Andrew's threat to expose him. Rather than face that, he was prepared to desert both the *Times* and his family.

"Why did you go there?"

She clenched her fists on her knees. "I was fed up. Things had been bad for a long time. No, that's wrong. They were always bad. Larry never cared about anything but that stupid paper. I didn't count, the kids didn't count, he screwed everything female that crossed his path. For years, I thought—well, this is how it is. But you can only put up with something for so long. Lately, I got to thinking maybe I didn't have to take this shit.

"I started bugging him to talk to me. At first, he barely paid attention. When I didn't shut up, he started promising we'd sit down and thrash the whole thing out. He'd say yes, and then he'd put it off. He'd have to work late, or he wasn't in the mood. I wouldn't get mad. I'd just say, 'Look, Larry, I'm going to have this out with you. When's it going to be?' We'd set another time, and it would happen all over again."

I could hardly breathe, feeling the weight of her frustration. "That night was the last time he promised," she went on. "I mean, here I was. Looking after the kids all day, zero money, while he went all over town playing big shot. Talking on the phone constantly, surrounded by girls telling him how great he was, while Zeke and Abner and I couldn't even afford to go to the movies.

"I was thinking, this is it. Decisions have to be made. He said he'd be here by seven-thirty. I got the kids off to bed early and sat down to wait. I wouldn't allow myself to do anything else. I sat here waiting.

"By eight-thirty, I knew in my gut he wasn't coming. I could've called, but I had done that so many times before, so I said, fuck it, I won't beg him to come home, but when he gets here he'd better watch out. And I sat and waited."

The memory seemed to animate her, and she got up and paced the room. "It must have been horrible," I said.

She turned toward me abruptly. "Horrible. It was horrible. About ten-thirty, I couldn't stand it any longer. I had reached the limit. So I went after him. I—this shows you the kind of mother I am. I left the kids here alone, asleep. They almost never wake up, you know, but suppose they had? Or what if the house had caught on fire? What a crazy, stupid thing to do!" There was intense anguish in the words. Susanna obviously felt more remorse for leaving her children alone at night than she did for killing Larry.

"But they didn't wake up, did they?" I was trying to offer comfort, but also to keep her talking.

"The times I've thought about how dumb that was." She sank to the floor and sat there, eyes tightly shut, clenched fist pressed against her mouth.

I crossed the room and helped her up. Her arm felt as thin as a child's. "Would you like some tea?" I asked, and she nodded and followed me into the kitchen. The kettle was on the stove, and I put water on to boil and found the teapot and some mugs in a cabinet.

She sat at the kitchen table. "Anyway, I got there," she said in a more normal tone. "I went up to his office and there he was. The window was open. He had some stuff on his desk. He was obviously feeling very hyper, and he wasn't pleased to see me."

I opened the tea canister. Lemon grass. No, Larry wouldn't have been pleased to see Susanna when he was worried about getting out of town before being exposed as a blackmailer.

"He said, 'What are you doing here?' as if I had no business to be there, no claim on his time, and that just made me madder. I asked him who the hell was he to say that, when he had promised to be home at seven-thirty, and he said, 'Oh, that,' as if it weren't important at all. And then, sounding very preoccupied, he said that he was going to leave town right now, because he was in a lot of trouble. He'd been planning to send me a note. A *note*!

"I said, 'What's going on?' and he said he didn't have time to explain, and I said I'd had enough of that shit, he was going to tell me or he wouldn't get out of there. I was standing in the doorway.

"He tried to push past me, and suddenly I felt so mad and so strong that I knew I wasn't going to let him go, and I shoved him back. I guess it took him by surprise, because he stumbled backwards a little, and I pushed him again and he fell against the desk. I grabbed the metal lamp off the desk and hit him on the head. It made a cut. Maybe I hit him a couple of times. It was like, you know, I couldn't stop myself. It felt good."

Her voice creaked a little, and I handed her a mug of tea. She took it without noticing. "He was bleeding a little and really scared by this time, and he was sort of scrambling backwards to get away from me. I felt strong and huge, like the strongest person in the world. I grabbed him when he was trying to get up, next to the window, and I said, 'Are you still leaving, Larry?' and he looked at me with this hate—real hate—in his face and he said, 'You bet I am, you bitch,' and he was about half-standing—" Susanna broke off. She shrugged. "I shoved him out the window," she said with a trace of surprise. "I shoved him and out he went, just like that. He didn't make a sound as he went down, and I heard him bounce off the garbage cans below. I wiped the lamp off and put it back on the desk and left."

I took my mug and sat down next to her at the table. She picked at its puckering, muddy yellow paint with her fingernail. "Let me ask you something," she said.

"What?"

"How did you realize it was me? The sheepskin jacket? I got rid of it after you were here and told me Richard had seen me."

"Not the jacket. The party hat."

She frowned. "Party hat?"

"When I was here yesterday, the dog was wearing a hat that said 'Pacific Bakery Anniversary Days' on it. When Richard told me about his gloves being stolen, he said there was a promotion going on when he stopped at Pacific Bakery Mall. Once I realized the two of you had crossed paths, it seemed obvious."

Susanna shook her head ruefully. "That silly hat was on the radio antenna of my car when I got back after taking Richard's gloves. I was so nervous I don't even remember, but I must have grabbed it and thrown it in the car. Bringing it in for the kids to play with was a reflex action."

We sat in silence. Then she put down her mug. "Now what?" she said.

I had been dreading the question. Susanna and I were so

much alike. Having been hurt, we had lashed back. Emotionally brutalized, we had discovered that we ourselves could be cruel. Would I perhaps have killed Richard, in Susanna's circumstances? The answer wasn't an unqualified no.

Yet Larry Hawkins had been alive. Death, I understood then, was more real than anything. More real than the table I sat at, the mug of tea I drank. I had felt it brush by me on three bullets tonight, and that had been too close. Bringing someone to that reality by force was wrong. I wanted to breathe, and move, and live out my time, and so had Larry.

"I'll have to call the police. I'm sorry."

She gnawed her lip. "You're sure?"

"Don't put me through this. It won't do any good. I've already mailed a letter to Andrew Baffrey telling him the whole story. It's too late."

She got up and walked toward the stove, then turned toward me pleadingly. "But a letter—a letter won't get there till tomorrow or the next day. The kids and I could be gone by then. If we started tonight, we could get away. I know we could."

She was standing in the corner where I had first seen her tonight, and again I saw her reach for the drawer. It came to me that she kept the gun there—a deadly weapon jumbled in with the napkins or the silverware. Her hand was on the knob. I had believed she didn't want to kill me, but now my body tensed, preparing to run for my life.

I stood up, holding my breath. She pulled out the drawer, almost casually.

A second later, she breathed deeply and closed the drawer with a thud. "It wouldn't work anyway," she said. "Both Zeke and Abner get miserably carsick on long trips. If you're going to call, you might as well do it now."

I went to the telephone.

THIRTY-FIVE

It was three in the morning when I got home. The past hours had been a blur of waiting, making sure somebody was looking after the Hawkins boys and the dog, drinking bitter coffee, and having a long session with Inspector Bosworth. The session included a chastening tirade on the value of allowing the police to do their jobs without being hampered by ex-wives and investigative reporters. Having already dealt with Andrew's accusation of Richard that evening, Bosworth was decidedly fed up by the time I came on the scene.

"Look, Mrs. Longstreet," he said. "If you get any more flashes like this, give me a call. Me personally. Don't try to do it yourself. You're goddam lucky you aren't dead, you know that?"

I knew that. I also knew there was a constricted feeling in my throat whenever I thought about Susanna Hawkins.

It didn't look as if anybody's friendship with the commissioner was going to prevent a complete investigation of the machinations surrounding the Golden State Center. Richard's phoenix would not rise, but would remain a stack of architect's drawings, cost analyses, and press releases.

I went over my story for the fourth or fifth time. I drank coffee. I signed the forms. At last, they told me I could leave. The sky was black, and a cold wind surged down the empty streets. Tears of depression and fatigue spilled out of my eyes and, too tired to wipe them away, I drove home with everything looking wavy and indistinct. Under the circumstances, it wasn't surprising that I had put the car in the garage and started up the front steps before I saw Andrew sitting at the top.

His legs were stretched out. In the dim glow from the streetlights almost all I could see were whitish blobs denoting his face and hands, and a glimmer from the dingy white laces of his running shoes. "Hi," he said. "I thought you were never coming home. Thought I was going to have to sit here all night."

I got out a tissue and blew my nose. "I see you made yourself comfortable."

"As best I could. I even caught a little nap, about half an hour ago."

"I was at the police station. Susanna killed Larry. I wrote you a letter telling about it, in case something happened to me."

"Actually, I heard. Part of the fallout from my proclaiming that Richard did it. I don't think Bosworth is too pleased with me."

"I don't think Bosworth is too pleased with either of us." I had reached the top step, and Andrew moved his legs out of my way. Sighing, I sat down beside him.

"You may be wondering what I've been thinking while I waited for you," he said.

"I assumed you might be thinking about how cold your rear end was getting."

"That, too. But mainly, Maggie, I was thinking how to apologize for being an unmitigated ass."

"Don't be so hard on yourself. Surely a mitigated ass is the worst you can claim."

"Will you forgive me for being a mitigated ass, then?"

"Sure." I hesitated. "Maybe I should ask you to forgive me for something, too."

"Great. I always hate it when the fault's all on one side. What have you done?"

I couldn't look at him. "Well, tonight—after we had our

fight and everything—I was casting around in my head for people who might've killed Larry, and I thought—"

"You thought maybe I did it?" He chuckled. "I was at a meeting of the Streets Committee that night. It started at eight and yawned on till past midnight. I was sitting in the front row. In other words, I've got a cast-iron alibi."

"Good. Now I won't have to be afraid to be alone with you."

He draped his arm around my shoulders. "I don't care what Bosworth says. If it weren't for us, none of this stuff would've come to light. We did a damn good job, even considering a few blunders here and there."

I leaned against him. "Damn good."

We sat for a while. The wind had died down to a breeze that ruffled our hair and stirred the branches of the Japanese magnolia. At last, we stood up, and I fumbled in my purse for my key.

About the Author

In a front-page article in *The New York Times Book Review*, Marilyn Stasio put Mickey Friedman among the new women detective fiction writers who are making an important impact on the genre. Stasio wrote that Friedman and others are "not only edging for professional places alongside their male counterparts, in some cases they are redefining the mystery genre by applying different sensibilities and values to it" ("Lady Gumshoes: Boiled Less Hard," April 28, 1985).

Mickey Friedman, a former San Francisco journalist, lives in New York City.

Attention Mystery and Suspense Fans

Do you want to complete your collection of mystery and suspense stories by some of your favorite authors? John D. MacDonald, Helen MacInnes, Dick Francis, Amanda Cross, Ruth Rendell, Alistar MacLean, Erle Stanley Gardner, Cornell Woolrich, among many others, are included in Ballantine/Fawcett's new Mystery Brochure.

For your FREE Mystery Brochure, fill in the coupon below and mail it to:

TA-94